ROUGH STOCK

CAT JOHNSON

Linden Bay Romance, LLC
Palm Harbor, Florida 34684
www.lindenbayromance.com

First Linden Bay Romance publication: December 2008

Thanks to all of my boot-wearing muses, be it cowboy or combat. I am especially grateful to Mike, the bull rider who rode to my rescue with the rodeo facts. And of course, to Sean and his squad for the Afghanistan battle scene details and the original idea to feature a rodeo cowboy turned soldier. Any inaccuracies or liberties taken with the facts in any of these arenas are strictly my own.

To my readers, thank you for supporting my first literary foray into both the ménage as well as the rodeo worlds. Let me know what you think! Email me anytime at cat.johnson@lindenbayromance.com.

PART I

Chapter One

The sudden appearance of pale, silky, feminine stomach stopped Clay Harris dead in his tracks. His greedy eyes devoured the smooth, firm skin, shadowed beneath the newfound lushness of her breasts.

He swallowed hard and found his voice husky. "April Elizabeth Carson. What do you think you're doing?"

She paused to look at him, one hand stopped in mid-motion as it tugged the hem of her shirt up over her bra—her white, thin, lacy bra. "What? It's hot. I'm going swimming."

Clay's best friend Mason Smith shot him a meaningful glance, a wide-eyed look of fear mingled with anticipation. "Um, shouldn't you go home and change into a suit first?" Mason suggested.

"Why? The house is so far and I'm hot now." Her

guileless pale blue eyes proved that she had not a single clue what she was doing to them.

Clay knew exactly what Mason was thinking when he made the suggestion about the swimsuit. Their good old buddy April who they'd met when they came to work for her father five years ago was hot all right, but not in the way she meant when she said it. She had filled out over the past school year. April had turned eighteen and suddenly transformed from an underweight, gangly teenage girl whom they had always treated like one of the guys into someone who was all female. One look at her and all of her new shapely curves and there was no denying it.

Clay swallowed hard. She was going to whip off her t-shirt and shorts and dive into that lake in nothing but her bra and underwear, like she had done at least once or twice each summer whenever the heat got unbearable. But this time, unlike the others, his raging eighteen-year-old male hormones would not be able to ignore it. Nor would she be able to ignore his hard-on, which was already starting to wake up just at the thought.

"Shit," Mason drawled out softly next to him as April did exactly as they feared, and what Clay suspected they both secretly wanted.

Stripped down to white bikini undies and the lace bra that looked nothing like last year's plain cotton tank-top style one, April pulled the elastic band out of her ponytail to release a tumbling cascade of long blond curls, and then dove into the clear lake water.

Hell, this was way better than sneaking peeks inside the skin magazines when the store clerk wasn't looking, but April was their friend. Now that she had suddenly turned into a woman, enjoying ogling her just seemed wrong, not to mention very weird.

Clay felt the already stifling Oklahoma heat around him ratchet up another notch. He wasn't convinced it had anything to do with the weather, even though it had never been quite this hot during the last week of the school year before. Now was a hell of a time for the weather to go wonky, Clay thought, as he and Mason watched April's progress.

She swam beneath the surface, gliding as easily as a fish through the water, before surfacing with a splash and a shake of her long, wet hair. Fish? Hell, she was more like a mermaid, and every man's wet dream.

"Aren't you two coming in?"

Hands buried deeply in both pockets, Mason surreptitiously adjusted himself within his jeans and glanced quickly at Clay. "Um, we need to get to the farm and start breaking that green horse your daddy just brought in or he's gonna tan our hides."

Barely comprehending Mason's excuse over his own lusty thoughts, Clay nodded in agreement with whatever his friend had just said.

"Fine. I'll get out. It's no fun swimming alone." With a pretty pout worthy of a centerfold, April stood, the water sluicing off satin skin that Clay longed to run his hands over, his tongue, too, while he was at it.

She began walking toward them, her water-soaked bra and panties so see-through, she might as well have been wearing nothing. Though somehow this was more enticing.

Clay swallowed again and nearly choked. He realized he had no spit in his mouth, even though he seemed to have plenty of sweat on his palms. He reached down and wiped them on the denim covering his thighs while what he really longed to do was reach down and adjust himself, because the seam of his stiff jeans was not doing his now wide-awake hard-on any good.

Before them, April bent over to grab her clothes off the grass, revealing the tops of two creamy breasts. Clay had barely noticed the plump globes above the scalloped edge of her bra before because he was too distracted by the dusky traces of her nipples through the wet material, not to mention the barely visible outline of the pale curls beneath her undies that proved she was all natural blond.

Mason hissed out a breath next to him. "Crap, Clay. This

4

just ain't right."

Clay didn't take his eyes off April as she dressed, wiggling and jumping to get her clothes on over wet skin. The act was somehow as enticing as a striptease, only in reverse. As April sat on the grass to pull her boots on, Clay asked, "What ain't right?"

Mason, the dark-haired, brown-eyed compliment to Clay's paler dirty blond, blue-eyed appearance, glowered. "You know damn well! She's our friend."

A quick sideways glance told Clay that in spite of his sudden moral protest, Mason hadn't taken his eyes off of April either. Clay grinned at him. "Yeah, but now she's our really hot female friend."

Mason finally broke his gaze from the sight that consumed them both to look at his buddy. He let out a resolution-filled sigh. "Yeah, she is, but how do you reckon we decide which one of us gets to take a shot at having her?"

Clay raised a brow. *Shit*. He hadn't considered that, but it was more than obvious, based on the physical evidence, that they both wanted her. Two of the Three Musketeers splitting off to be a couple while the third stood by and watched was not going to work well for the group dynamic.

"What are you two whispering about?" Suddenly, April was beside them, her still loose hair dripping down her back and over her shoulders, insuring that her white t-shirt stayed nice and wet and translucent just a little bit longer before the summer sun dried it and ruined the view.

"Nothing. Come on. I can't wait to get my hands on that new stock." Lying to her, Clay realized the new horse wasn't the only thing he couldn't wait to get his hands on.

He also realized that turning a good friendship with April into an even better one would surely be nice, but losing his best friend Mason in the process would suck.

One last thought crossed his mind as his pants felt tighter than ever. Riding a horse with a hard-on was going to really suck, too. Clay sincerely hoped his dick went down before he had to get up in the saddle or he'd be one unhappy cowboy. Next to him, Mason pulled his hat lower over his eyes and concentrated overly hard on the ground at his boots. Clay would bet this week's paycheck from April's daddy that Mason was thinking the exact same thing. They both had better rein in their hormones.

"Clinton asked me to go to the prom with him next week."

At April's announcement, Clay tripped over the toe of his boot and came to a sudden, jolting stop in the road, Mason nearly running into the back of him.

Clinton was the quarterback of their high school football team, on top of having a rich daddy and a full-ride athletic scholarship to one of the big schools back east. He had everything cowboys like Clay and Mason, who worked for a living and couldn't afford college, didn't have. Clay would handle losing April to Mason if it came down to it, but he'd be damned before he let Clinton get April on top of everything else the privileged ass already had.

He tried to make his voice sound casual. "What'd you say to him?"

April shrugged. "I told him I'd give him an answer tomorrow."

Mason gave his hat a shove backwards so he could look April in the eye. "What are you going to tell him?"

Yeah, Mason was no happier about this than Clay. Even if April hadn't suddenly turned into a hottie they wanted for themselves, Clay still wouldn't want her anywhere near Clinton. The guy had a hell of a reputation as a womanizer already, and he had only just turned eighteen. Clinton took after his daddy, if rumors were anything to go by. Clay knew that usually there was a bit of truth in even the most outrageous gossip. It was hard to keep a secret in a small community like theirs.

April looked from one boy to the other. "I'll probably say yes since you guys aren't going, right?"

Mason frowned beneath the brim of his hat. "We can't. You know we're both signed up to ride in the rough stock competition in Elk City that day. It's the big championship."

Clay nodded. "Yeah, we assumed you'd be coming to Elk City. You know, to watch us ride, like you usually do."

April's face fell a bit. "You guys ride in every rodeo within driving distance. I can come and see you anytime. But the prom…that's once in a lifetime. You know? I kind of wanted to go."

She scuffed the toe of her boot against the ground and Clay couldn't help but notice exactly how sexy the long, lean muscles of her legs looked in those denim cut-offs and boots. The discussion about Clinton had momentarily deflated his formerly happy erection, but the view was stirring things up again.

"I thought maybe if you two wanted, we could all go to the prom together." April watched both he and Mason expectantly.

Why hadn't she told them before now that she had suddenly become a sentimental girly girl who would choose a prom over a rodeo? *Shit.*

Clay frowned. "Mason and I already paid the entry fee." Nearly half a week's pay for each of them, but it was worth it. The purse, if either of them won, would way more than make up for what it had cost them in the entry fees and food stops while they were on the road.

"And your father is supplying rough stock for the amateur division. He's counting on us driving the horse trailer out for him 'cause he and your mama have plans that night."

"Then I'll tell Clinton I'll go with him. No problem." She turned on her heel and started down the road again.

Clay jogged after her. "Now, don't get all mad at us, April."

"I'm not." She shot him a look that belied what she said.

Clay huffed out a breath in frustration. "If you had told us you wanted to go before we signed up and paid for the competition, maybe we might have gone with you to the stupid prom instead."

Her stiffened spine as she walked on ahead told him he hadn't made things any better.

Shaking his head with a scowl, Mason shot Clay a look that had the word *idiot* written all over it and stepped faster after April.

Buckets of bull crap. Clay ran after them, regretting that April had grown up. If this new and wonderful woman's body came packaged with the typical female inexplicable weirdness and perplexing behavior, he could do without it. He missed that she was no longer just one of the guys. Then he looked up and noticed her nicely rounded butt cheeks jiggling temptingly within her shorts as she angrily stomped down the road and he changed his mind.

When they reached her daddy's farm, she broke off from

them with barely a goodbye and headed for the house, while he and Mason turned toward the barns.

"Way to piss her off there, Clay."

Glancing up, Clay noticed Mason was smiling. "What the hell are you smiling about? We're both going to Elk City instead of with her to that prom."

Still grinning, Mason grabbed a lead rope from the wall. "Yeah, but I didn't call the prom stupid, genius."

Following Mason to the paddock where the new horse had been turned out, Clay scowled. Calling it a stupid prom probably hadn't been the smartest thing he'd done in recent memory, but he wasn't going to let Mason get away with assuming his chances with April were any better than Clay's.

"Hate to burst your bubble there, buddy, but it's not me you have to worry about. Clinton's daddy can buy and sell both our families with what he's got in his wallet alone. You think that's not going to turn her head? Shit. She goes with him and we can write off any hope either one of us had with her for anything more than just friendship."

Mason stopped with his hand on the gate. "Jeez, Clay! Give her some credit. She's not stupid and her head won't be turned by money. She wants to go to the prom, that's all. So let Clinton foot the bill and take her. But I tell you what, a few hours of being with him and she'll come running back to us."

Clay raised a brow. "You think?"

"Hell yeah! Did you ever hear that sissy pretty boy jock talk about anything besides football or that new sports car Daddy bought him?"

Clay thought for a second and then grinned. "You know what? I can't say I have."

April loved two things, horses and reading books. Football and cars weren't going to get Clinton into that girl's pretty white panties, or anywhere else.

With renewed hope, Clay swung the gate open and got ready for some good old-fashioned horse breaking, knowing that the minute he and Mason had the new horse in the ring, April would be down there. Pissed or not, the girl couldn't resist watching them break a horse.

Clay let his mind stray to how he'd love to break April in, until a handful of spirited, rearing horse demanded all of his attention as he jumped to help Mason.

Chapter Two

Mason grunted as the horse circled the ring with him laying belly down across its back with nothing but a saddle blanket to cushion his stomach as he got jostled during a brisk trot.

Whether saddle horses for riding like this one, or bucking broncos for rough stock competitions, Mason loved training horses. He knew Clay more than loved it. He lived for it. However, this particular part, Mason could probably live without. Get him up in a saddle and he was happy, but this step in the training process, though brief, just plain sucked.

The new gelding, after many hours and many days of gentle persuading, had taken to them putting a folded blanket over his back. He'd even, after a bit of bucking, let them hang two sandbags over him so he'd get used to the feel of weight on his back and sides. And since Clay had been the one to hop up and lay across the back of the last horse they'd broken, it was Mason's turn today. *Oh, goody.*

But things were going well so far. The horse hadn't taken off galloping with Mason, nor had he tried to buck him off. That was exactly the results they wanted. They were one step closer to getting a saddle up on him and making him a valuable saddle horse, or maybe even a barrel horse, for April's daddy. Of course, tightening down the cinch on a green horse's belly was the challenge, more than just throwing on the saddle. Then, once he got used to the empty saddle on him, they would try a rider.

One step at a time. Right now, Mason had to worry more about losing his lunch. Next time he'd remember not to go up for seconds of the school cafeteria Sloppy Joes before doing this shit.

Clay stood in the center of the ring, controlling the horse on a lunge line. The colt had been trotting for long enough that Mason could feel the horse's labored breathing beneath him and see the sweat lathering his flank.

"Hold up, Clay."

Taking a step forward, Clay shortened the lunge line and slowed the horse. "Ho, there. Ho."

Jumping clear, Mason tried not to stumble even though his equilibrium was shot to hell after that face down belly ride. "He's had enough for today. It's too damn hot to keep working him."

Clay nodded and strode up to the horse to unhook the long lunge line from his halter as Mason took out his bandana and mopped his face. The horse wasn't the only one sweating in this heat. Only difference was, Mason could guzzle some water, the horse would have to wait until he cooled off a bit first or they risked shocking his system.

Heading for the spot where he'd dropped his water bottle before, Mason's face broke out into a smile as he spotted April sitting in the shade behind a big oak tree, probably hoping they wouldn't notice her.

Mason swung over the top rail of the ring, grabbed the bottle and took a gulp of now tepid water as Clay joined him.

"Well, well. Do you see who I see?" Clay grinned, grabbing his own bottle of water.

He swallowed another mouthful of water and nodded. "Yup, I sure do."

"Humph. I knew she couldn't stay away from the horses, pissed at us or not."

"Pissed at *you,* my friend. Not me."

Clay shook his head. "You know damn well she's not just upset I called the prom stupid, which it is. She's mad because you and I didn't drop out of the competition to go with her."

Mason considered that theory. "Maybe." He laughed at himself and what he was about to say next. "Maybe we should."

Clay shot him a look of disbelief. "That entry fee cost us practically half a week's pay each! We'd forfeit that and have to buy tickets to the stupid prom."

"I know. But if it makes her happy..."

Clay shook his head and sighed. "You are thinking with your little head now."

Maybe, but Mason was sure he wasn't the only one. "As if you haven't been drooling over her since the second she stripped off her clothes this afternoon and jumped in that pond."

The image of April standing before them, beautiful and totally unaware of what torture she was inflicting on two horny teenage boys, filled his brain until Clay interrupted his thoughts.

"I never said I wasn't drooling. We both were. But the purse in Elk City will be huge and there will be a lot of big names riding. If we were gonna skip a competition to dress up like fools and pay a bunch of money to go to some dance, this is not the competition to drop out of and you know it. She'll get over it. Don't worry. Like you said, next to that ass Clinton, we both will look like Prince Charming."

Mason was covered in dust and smelled like a mixture of

sweat, wet wool blanket, and horseflesh. *Prince Charming*? Not quite. "Let's not push it. And shush up now 'cause she's coming."

He watched April stand, leave her shaded hiding spot and make her way over to them.

Clay glanced over his shoulder and cringed when he saw the determined look on her face. "I'm, ah, gonna go ask if they want him turned out in the paddock or put back in the barn after we hose him off."

Mason grinned. "Chicken."

He heard Clay making soft clucking noises as he walked away and laughed, until April was closer and that not so happy look was turned on him now.

She watched the still high-strung horse pace back and forth, from one side of the ring to the other. "I wanna ride him."

Mason watched her rather than the horse. "He's coming along good. I think in a few weeks, after we've been up on him a few times, I'm sure your daddy will agree if we let you hop on him in the ring."

April shook her head and turned to face Mason. "No. I mean I want to ride him now."

Mason was sure the look on his face told her what he thought about that idea. "April, we haven't even gotten a saddle on him yet."

"So? I can ride bareback."

That statement popped a very ungentlemanly, though tantalizing image into his head. Damn! If Mason kept picturing April naked as she rode *him* in her bed, he'd be forfeiting that entrance fee and putting on his dancing boots before he knew it.

Remembering Clay, Mason shook the crazy thought from his head. Clay would really be pissed at him if he dropped out and let him go ride alone. As much as Mason wanted more with April, the consequences of choosing her over Clay was not something he cared to consider.

He'd have to figure something out. In the meantime, what was with her wanting to ride the green horse? "No. I won't let you up on him until he's saddle broken. You could get hurt."

"Like you'd care."

It was mumbled under her breath, but Mason heard it just fine. Maybe Clay was right. She was mad because they hadn't dropped out of the competition to take her to the prom. As if their willingness to do *that* was any indication of what good friends they were.

Mason raised his hand, noticed that it was much too dirty and sweaty to be touching the smooth creamy skin of her pretty face and instead laid it on her shoulder. "I care very much, April. It would kill me if anything happened to

17

you."

April watched him with a narrowed glare before breaking eye contact and letting out a big sigh. "Maybe you care, but he doesn't." She cocked a head in the direction that Clay had gone.

Mason paused, biting his tongue.

Damn. It was most likely stupid to defend his number one competition for this girl when it looked like he was in the lead, but Clay was his best friend, closer than a brother, and Mason had to tell the truth. "You know that's not true. He cares as much as I do."

Mason noticed he had absently begun playing with one curl that had escaped from her ponytail and dangled on her shoulder. He swallowed hard and let the curl as well as his hand drop.

Touching her was too damn tempting. He could feel the heat radiating off her body, and he wasn't convinced it was just from the unseasonable weather.

Mason considered exactly when it had happened, this sudden awareness of April as more than just a friend. Certainly it hadn't been overnight, so why the hell hadn't he noticed she affected him like this until now? It seemed as if one day she was just April, his and Clay's buddy who tagged along fishing and watched them ride, and then WHAM! She was April, the girl with the body who wanted to go to the

18

prom and almost made him want to also. Almost.

"Look, April, about this prom…"

She cut him off. "It's not a problem, Mason. I just thought it would be more fun to go with you two, but I already called Clinton and told him I'll go with him. So it's done. See? All taken care of. You two can ride your broncos, and I get to go to the prom. Everyone's happy."

Yeah, right. Not by a long shot. "You are not happy," Mason observed. And the thought of her dancing in Clinton's arms didn't make him too happy, either.

She tilted her head to one side and shrugged. "I'm fine."

Mason sighed. "If you had just told us sooner, maybe…"

"I know. It's okay, Mason. Really. I am fine. It's just one night. You guys do your thing, and I'll do mine, then we can tell each other about it the next day."

He considered her new nonchalant attitude. "You sure?"

April nodded and even forced a smile. "Positive."

If only Mason was so sure.

Chapter Three

"You think that damn prom is over yet?" Clay backed the Carson's trailer up to the barn so they could unload the horses.

Mason shrugged. "Ain't no telling."

Clay twisted in the driver's seat to peer past Mason at the house. "The front light's still on. That means she's not home yet." He glanced at the clock on the dashboard. "At nearly one o'clock in the damn morning."

Not liking that fact or the implications himself, Mason opened the truck door. "Let's get these horses unloaded before we get to worrying about her. Okay?"

Still looking unhappy, Clay gave in and nodded.

They got the horses to bed, but they did it while both of them silently worried about where April was and what she and Clinton were doing. And then they were done, and Clay was staring at the house again. "I think we should wait for her to get home."

"I agree." Mason was sore, tired and he stunk. Yet he still nodded and, arms folded, settled himself on a bale of hay for the duration.

They didn't have long to wait. He heard her before he saw her. When she did come into view, sobbing and limping down the road, Mason wasn't sure who moved first, but both he and Clay got to her in a split second.

Clay touched the shoulder of her torn white dress. The light from the front porch reached to where they stood and Mason saw the look his friend shot him. Mason knew Clay was thinking the same thing he was—if Clinton did this to April, they'd make sure he paid for it, and not with his daddy's money, either. Mason had other ideas.

Jaw set, Mason tried to speak gently so as not to frighten her any more. The poor thing was already shaking so badly it was a miracle she was still on her feet. "April, what happened tonight?"

She shook her head and released another huge sob.

Clay wrapped his arm around her and she pressed her face into his chest, clinging to him. "Shhh. It's okay now. We're here." Clay shot another worried glance at Mason past the top of her quivering head.

Mason took the opportunity to look her over better now that she couldn't see him doing it, and he didn't like what he found one bit. Her shoes were missing and her feet looked dirty and blood-smeared, like she'd walked a long way. Besides the shoulder of her dress being torn, it looked like her hair had been fastened up at the start of the night, but it was pulled halfway down now. Then he moved and the light struck her arms. He saw the bruises forming there. Someone had manhandled April and he had a very good idea who it was.

Angry now, Mason pulled her away from Clay's chest, one hand holding her chin as he inspected her face. Besides her tears, which broke his heart and fueled his mad, her lip was split open and bleeding. "Did Clinton do this?"

Still shaking and sobbing, she finally nodded.

Dropping his hold on her, Mason spun on the heel of his boot and headed for the truck. He heard Clay behind him. "Wait up. I'm coming with you."

"You should stay with April."

"And let you go alone to take care of Clinton? To hell with that. She's my friend, too. We both beat the crap out of him then we come back here and make sure she's all right. I told her to leave her window open and expect us in an hour."

Mason nodded and walked around to the driver's side of the truck, which, technically, since they'd only been asked to

22

drive it to Elk City and back, they were now stealing. He didn't think April's daddy would mind if he knew why they needed it. Hell, he'd probably grab his rifle and come with them.

Turning the key in the ignition, Mason did his best to control himself and not slam on the accelerator and peel out of the gravel drive. "You told her an hour?"

Clay nodded.

"I don't know if an hour of kicking his ass is going to be enough to get this mad out of my system."

Holding on to the door handle as Mason took the turn out of the drive a bit too fast, Clay turned to look at him. "It's gonna have to be. April needs us."

And that would be the only thing that could drag Mason away from taking his size elevens and kicking that rotten, rich boy bastard until the sun came up.

They found Clinton pretty much where they expected him to be, outside in the park, drinking, his car easy to spot where it was parked along the curb. When Daddy owned half the town, the cops tended to turn a blind eye to his son's underage drinking with his usual entourage. That was one reason Mason never even considered having April call the police about what Clinton had done. The law in this town could be bought and sold, but justice in this case would not be, not if Mason had anything to say about it.

23

Judging by the look on Clinton's face, and that of his two scum friends, they knew exactly why Clay and Mason pulled the horse truck up to the curb and jumped out. And yet the bastard still had the nerve to grin and elbow his friend next to him. "Look, if it isn't April's two boyfriends. I thought I smelled horse shit."

"There's three of them," Clay said softly next to him.

Mason nodded. "And they're drunker than shit, so don't worry about it." Besides, Mason was mad enough to take them on all alone.

Clay cracked his knuckles and took another step forward. "Oh, I'm not worried. I'm just wondering which one of us gets the pleasure of kicking two asses instead of just one."

Mason matched Clay step for agonizingly slow step as they got closer to their prey. "I tell you what. You let me take Clinton and you can have the other two all to yourself."

"Well, now, that's not fair. I wanted Clinton."

Mason was very well aware that Clinton and his cronies could hear every word, and yet still the bastards grinned like they'd gotten away with something.

After taking one final step, Mason stopped right in front of Clinton. "You know what? You are really starting to piss me off." And with that, he swung all of his body weight into his fist and watched the blood and spit fly as Clinton's head whipped to the side and he landed on his ass in the grass.

They needn't have worried about who got to take on the other two, because they took one look at the punch Mason had thrown and began backing up, wide-eyed.

Mason grinned. "Hmm. Looks like you're on your own there, Clinton."

"Well, shit. Now it's gonna look bad. Two of us beating the shit out of only one of them." Clay pointed at one of the two retreating guys. "You. Come on back here and take a swing at me so it's a fair fight and I get my chance at Clinton, too."

"I wouldn't worry about fair, Clay. Any man who hits a woman forfeits rights to a fair fight." Teeth clenched tight, Mason pulled back for another punch. "Stand up, coward."

Still on his ass on the ground, Clinton scrambled backwards a few feet, like a cowardly crab crawling toward the safety of the surf.

"She only got what was coming to her. Thinking I'm going pay for her to go to the prom and she's not going to put out. The girl's a cock tease. Acting all like she's a virgin or something when everyone around here knows you two have both been diddling with her for years now."

"Oh, that's it. Move out of the way, Mason." Clay was on Clinton like a lion on a fresh piece of meat, hauling him up off the grass only to slam him up against a tree. "Now, you take that back about April."

A few smashes of his head against the trunk and Clinton was crying, which was when Clay let him drop with a snort of disgust. "You ain't worth it. Let's go, Mason."

Some men were just too stupid to know when to keep their mouths shut. Apparently, Clinton was one of them. As Clay turned his back on him, the idiot couldn't leave well enough alone. "You two run on back and fuck your whore, but I sure hope you don't mind getting my sloppy seconds."

From that point on it was hard to tell whose fists were whose. All Mason knew was that Clay finally grabbed him. "Mason. Enough."

With another glance at Clinton's bloodied face, Mason let Clay steer him back to the truck and shove him into the passenger's side door.

Enough time had been wasted on that lowlife Clinton. April needed them now.

As Clay started the truck, Mason realized Clay was right to stop him. They'd do April no good if they were in jail. But shit. What Clinton had said he'd done to her nearly ate a hole in Mason's gut.

"Clay. What if what he said was true. What if he…" Mason couldn't bring himself to say the word rape.

Feeling the truck accelerate, Mason watched Clay's throat work as he swallowed hard, his friend's eyes never leaving the road as he avoided answering the question. "We'll be there in a minute."

Mason felt his own heart pounding at the thought. "And…then what?"

Clay looked at him now, for too long considering the speed at which the truck was hurtling down the dark road. "We take her to the hospital to get looked at, and then we go back and kill him."

Mason nodded. He could live with that.

Clay didn't slow down until they had arrived back at April's farm, then, he steered the truck down the drive as slowly and quietly as he could, but still, the sound of the tires crunching on the gravel sounded deafeningly loud in the darkness, cutting the silence typical of the middle of the night.

The two swung their doors shut slowly, pushing them until they barely latched to avoid any more noise that might wake April's parents.

The front porch light had been turned off. Mason hoped April had done that on her way in and that her parents were still sleeping soundly, unaware of the two cowboys about to crawl through their bruised and battered daughter's bedroom window.

This wouldn't be the first time they'd done this. Not for the purpose that Clinton had accused them of, but kids will be kids, and they had been sneaking in, or helping April sneak out, for years now. Sometimes they'd all go night fishing. More recently, they'd grab a six-pack of beer and the three of them would sit by the lake and talk.

Tonight would be the first time Mason absolutely dreaded talking to April. He really didn't want to hear the answer to the question they were about to ask her. Judging by the look of her when she'd come hobbling down the road, and from Clinton's bragging, Mason feared he already knew the answer.

She had left the window open, just as Clay asked her to, and all Mason had to do was hop up on the sill and swing a leg inside.

April had changed out of the torn dress and was wrapped in an extra large t-shirt and her top sheet, in spite of the heat. She sat upright in the bed, hugging her knees and rocking, until she saw Mason coming through the window. "Oh, thank god. I was so worried. What did you two do?"

She was worried about *them*?

Clay was over the windowsill and next to him in an instant and they both went to sit on either side of her on the bed. Clay answered her question. "We had to take care of some garbage. How are you feeling, darlin'?"

"Better." Her voice sounded breathy in the darkness.

Mason ran one hand gently down her arm, careful not to

hurt the bruises he knew were there but couldn't see in the room lit only by a tiny nightlight in one corner. He had to ask her this, though he didn't want to. "I need you to tell us what happened, April."

She shook her head, silent.

Clay laid one hand on her sheet-covered knee. "You need to, darlin'. It's important."

"He just…tried stuff. That's all. Nothing happened."

Mason swallowed and kept rubbing her arm, more for his comfort than for hers at this point.

"April, baby." Mason cleared his throat and began again. "It's us. You can tell us anything. You know that. And we know that whatever happened tonight, he forced on you. But you have to tell us if you two had sex because we have to take care of you if you did."

"No!" April jerked back from him and her denial came out a bit too loudly.

As happy as the answer made him, Mason, and Clay too, shushed her before her parents woke up.

She lowered her voice and repeated, "No."

"The truth?" Clay asked, mirroring what Mason wanted to ask.

"Yes, the truth! I kneed him the way you guys taught me years ago. When he was bent over in pain in that car he loves so much, I got out and ran home."

29

Clay laughed out loud. Mason allowed himself a small smile, thankful that two thirteen-year-old boys had had the sense to teach a young April self-defense.

He heard Clay release a loud breath as he gathered April in a big hug. "I am very happy to hear that. I would have really hated to have to go back and kill him."

"Would you really have done that?" April asked, sounding so incredibly small.

Mason answered her question before Clay, his voice flat and matter of fact. "Yes."

She turned in Clay's arms to face Mason. "Why?"

That answer was easy. "Because we care about you. A lot."

April reached out and touched his face softly. "I care about you both, too."

Clay laughed on the other side of her. "As it is, Clinton's not going to be looking so pretty for the graduation ceremony next week."

"Did you hurt him really bad?"

"Um…" Clay hesitated. Mason didn't.

"Yes, we did. You okay with that?"

April thought for a second. "I may be a horrible person to say this but, yes, I am okay with that."

She flopped backwards to lie against her pillow. With one booted foot each still on the floor, Clay and Mason followed, each one lying on his side next to her.

They'd lain like this many times before when they would stay up half the night talking and then fall asleep in her bed, only to sneak out at dawn and pretend to be just arriving to see to the horses' morning feeding.

"He kept saying he knew that I...that we..." April couldn't finish the sentence.

Clay nodded and put one finger across her lips. "Shhh, it's okay. We know. He said the same shit to us."

"People are idiots. You can't listen to what he said, to what anybody says." Mason reached out and played with one of her curls that lay near his face on the pillow.

"Yeah, I know." April let out a huge sigh and then laughed sadly. "You both stink like horse. Did you at least win?"

"I did and I've got the prize money and the buckle in my saddlebag to prove it." Mason could hear the pride in Clay's voice.

"Mason? What about you?"

Clay answered that question for him. "He ended up eating a face full of dirt."

Mason scowled. "Thanks, Clay."

April squeezed his arm comfortingly and then they were all silent for a bit. Mason thought maybe she'd fallen asleep, until her soft voice filled the darkness once again. "I've thought about it, you know."

Clay kicked off his boots so that they landed on the floor with a thud, then swung both his feet up onto the bed. "Thought about what, darlin'?"

Figuring they were here for the night since sunrise was only a few hours away, Mason had just let his own boots drop to the floor so he could get comfortable when April answered.

"I've thought about us being together...like that. The three of us."

She stared straight up at the ceiling as she let that bomb drop on them both.

For once, even Clay was speechless. All Mason heard come out of his friend was a soft shocked wheeze of air at April's comment. She'd said it so casually, as if she hadn't just blurted out the most outrageous, tantalizing thing Mason had ever heard in all of his eighteen years.

He realized just how close their three faces were. So close, that when she turned her head slightly on the pillow, her breath tickled his nose. Her hand came up to pull Mason's head even closer. She kissed him softly on the lips.

Then, as Mason's heart pounded with the possibilities, April turned her head and he saw her plant the same soft kiss on Clay. Only Clay wasn't as polite, or perhaps not as shocked, as Mason had been. It took barely a second before

Clay tangled his hand in her hair, tilted his head and kissed her deeper, just inches from Mason's face. He watched his two best friends kiss, amazed, aroused, confused…

As their tongues tangled and Clay let out a small moan, Mason began to wonder what the hell to do. Should he leave? Stay? Join in? Mason moved on the bed, sitting up, unsure until April blindly grabbed his denim-clad thigh with one hand and held him there. Her touch sent shockwaves through his body, directly into his now rock hard erection.

She broke the kiss with Clay and turned her head back to him. In the dim light, Mason saw her lick her lips before she leaned in. Then the tip of that tongue he'd watched dart out of her mouth just seconds before, was parting his own lips. Her mouth was hot and wet and tasted of toothpaste.

His eyes still open so he wouldn't miss one moment, Mason saw Clay's hand snake around from behind her to cup April's breast through her t-shirt.

If Clay wasn't fighting this, he sure as hell wasn't going to. With one hand stroking April's bare leg from knee to thigh, Mason let his eyes drift closed to enjoy the intimacy, if not privacy, of their first real kiss together.

Mason sensed as, very near to his face, Clay moved April's hair, kissing her neck from behind. She let out a soft moan that Mason felt vibrate through her kiss and into him.

Mason let his hand move slowly higher, traveling up the

length of smooth skin at the back of her leg, until he encountered the elastic of her panties. He dipped a fingertip beneath the band, playing with the soft warm crease just below the curve of her ass, afraid to move too fast after what she'd already been through that night.

April bent one knee, spreading her legs in open invitation for his hand to explore further. He longed to plunge a finger inside her and touch what he knew would be hot and heavenly, but he hesitated. It was probably too soon for that.

He regretfully moved his hand away from the temptation and brought it up to cup her face as he plunged his tongue deeper into her mouth.

Feeling the bed shift, Mason drew a shaky breath in through his nose as April's kiss became rougher. When Mason broke the kiss and opened his eyes, he realized the reason why. He saw that Clay was now on his knees at the foot of the bed, pulling April's panties down and off so he could spread her thighs further apart and kneel between them.

Clay dipped his head low. April's body jolted and Mason knew exactly what his friend was doing to her.

Mason watched her squeeze her eyes shut and press her head back against the pillow. Nearly immobilized with fascination, he looked down to watch his best friend's hands part April's lips as his tongue darted out to tease her. Her body twitched in response as she drew in a quick shaky breath that hardened him even further, as if that was possible.

Swallowing hard, Mason pulled April's oversized t-shirt up and over her head and lowered his own head to draw one peaked nipple into his mouth. He scraped it gently with his teeth as, with a shuddering sigh, she pushed her breast higher to press more deeply into his mouth. He gave the other peak equal attention and then turned greedily back to her mouth as her breaths came faster and small sounds that cut straight through to his core came from deep in her throat.

While his fingers took over to work one aroused nipple, Mason thrust his tongue into her mouth. He felt her hips rise off the bed as he kissed her deeper. Still joined at the lips, Mason opened his eyes and looked down at Clay again. He felt his balls tighten as he watched Clay work April with his tongue and both hands.

Wrapping one arm more tightly around her, Mason groaned himself as he felt April get more aroused, nearing closer to orgasm.

Whatever Clay was doing, worked. Only Mason's mouth being on hers muffled the sound as April cried out, hips thrusting as her one hand grabbed blindly at Clay's head, holding him tighter against her.

Feeling April come apart in his arms was nearly enough to make Mason come himself. Nearly, but not quite. He was so hard he throbbed, feeling every beat of his pulse vibrate through his cock.

She finally began to quiet, pushed Clay away and broke from Mason's mouth. She lay back, breathing as hard as if she'd run a marathon. Mason glanced down and saw Clay grin while wiping his mouth with the back of his hand.

Unable to face the reality of this just yet, Mason flopped back onto the pillow and threw his free forearm over his face. April's head still lay on his right arm, pinning it beneath her.

Mason was just trying to slow his own breathing and heartbeat when he felt Clay crawl back up the bed to lie on the other side of April. One hard muscular arm came flying over April's nude and still gasping body to accidentally land on Mason's jean-covered leg. At that point, Mason realized exactly how entwined the three of them now were, and he wasn't just talking the tangle of limbs in the bed, either.

Chapter Four

Clay woke about dawn, still fully dressed and not nearly rested. As his brain slowly came into focus, memories of last night flooded back, making his morning hard-on even harder than usual from being neglected for so long. It currently nestled against the temptingly bare crevice of April's ass, the thickness of the denim of his jeans between them not nearly enough. She was turned away from him, sleeping on Mason's chest. Clay heard both of their breathing, even and measured in sleep.

If Clay were less of a gentleman, he'd take advantage of his position. All he needed to do was lower his zipper and slide into what he had felt first hand was hot, wet, and wonderful.

He pictured what they'd done together last night and

decided he better not use that term *gentleman* again in reference to himself for a little bit. He'd had both his tongue and his fingers inside of a girl he not only cared a lot about both as a friend and more, but who he knew was a virgin, all while his best friend had his own tongue down her throat while playing with her tits. Not exactly gentlemanly on either of their parts.

Clay gingerly pulled back both the arm and leg he'd thrown across her body in his sleep and rose, as quietly as he could, from the bed. It was Sunday. April's parents would be waking up to leave for church service soon, but Clay had to pee. Short of aiming out the window, he figured he'd be safe enough slipping into the hall bathroom since her parents had their own bathroom at the other end of the house.

Thank goodness the master bedroom was on the opposite side in a wing past the kitchen. That architectural configuration had made it easy for them to sneak through the window for many late night talks in April's room for many years now. Clay would remember that when designing his own house in case he ever had a daughter of his own. His daughter's room would be right next to his, possibly guarded by a big dog to prevent any boys slipping in and doing to his future daughter exactly what they'd done to April last night.

With that surreal image filling his brain, Clay opened April's door slowly, carefully, and peered out into the hall.

From his muffled position between April's legs last night, he couldn't be sure how loud the three of them had gotten. Though he supposed if her parents had heard, they would have been in her bedroom long before now. That would be all Clay needed, her daddy in his face with a shotgun for taking advantage of his only daughter.

Peeing took longer than usual due to the rock-hard, April-induced erection that refused to go down. By the time he got back to the bedroom, he saw Mason's eyes were open.

"We should get out of here," Clay mouthed to him.

Mason nodded. Glancing down at April's head, he slowly pulled his body out from beneath her.

Clay bent to retrieve his boots and pulled them on as Mason did the same and joined him by the window saying, "Poor thing is exhausted. She didn't even wake up."

Clay glanced back at the still sleeping figure on the bed. At some point in the night, she'd pulled her t-shirt back on, so at least she wasn't nude in case her parents came in to wake her. Then he noticed for the first time the bruises on her arms and the split in her lip. It had been too dark last night for him to see them.

Angry all over again, he slid over the windowsill, jumped to the ground and strode fast toward the barns before he blew up within earshot of the house. When Mason caught up to him, Clay stopped next to the paddock, spun and mouthed a foul curse. "Did you see those bruises on her?"

Mason nodded as he unzipped his jeans and relieved himself with a long morning piss on a fence post. "I saw them last night, right before I got into the truck intent on killing Clinton."

Clay remembered that portion of the evening with as much fondness as what had happened later. "He deserved what we gave him and more."

Zipped up again, Mason bent to grab the hose to wash his hands and face before he rinsed his mouth with the fresh water. Clay was feeling a bit grimy himself after a night spent in his clothes. He could use a shower and some toothpaste, but this would do for now. He took his turn at the hose as Mason said, "You think he'll press charges?"

Clay finished up and turned off the water. "Against us? When she can press charges against him for attempted rape? No way."

"It was two against one."

"It was three against two. Not our fault his friends are chicken shit. Even then, we played fair. We took him on one at a time until he said that shit about April. After that...well, he's lucky to be alive."

Mason nodded. "Thanks for pulling me off him."

Clay grinned. "No problem, man. That's what friends are for. We're a team." His mind went back to what else they had done as a team the night before and shook his head in amazement at the memory. "Last night." He let out a short laugh. "Mason, that was something."

Mason let out a wry laugh and glanced back at the house. "Yeah, but I wonder how she's going to feel about it in the light of day."

Clay frowned. "Why would the sun being up change a thing?"

"You know damn well that things that seem like a good idea at the time look stupid as shit the next day. Like the night you emptied your daddy's liquor cabinet and threw me a birthday party down by the lake."

Clay couldn't sit down for a week after the beating he'd gotten over that stunt, but he certainly hoped Mason was wrong about April, because last night was just the beginning of all that he wanted to do with her.

He shook his head in denial. "Nah. She started it by kissing us. She'll be okay."

Mason raised a brow. "She kissed us both like a friend. You shoved your tongue in her mouth."

Clay scowled. "I didn't *shove*. I'm not Clinton. I don't force myself on women. You know I would have stopped right away if she wanted me to. Did you see her complaining?"

Mason kicked at the dirt with the toe of his boot. "No."

"So, then she'll be fine."

Mason looked skeptical. "We'll see."

"Yes, we will. And stop worrying about everything. *Will Clinton press charges? Will April regret last night?* You sound like an old woman or something." Clay was a natural optimist and he hated when Mason, Mr. Glass-Half-Empty, continuously burst his bubble.

Mason scowled at Clay. "Yeah, well while you're making lists of my worries, let me add something to it. After last night, I've been rethinking our plans for the future. About us turning pro and riding on the PRCA circuit."

"Why? What's us being with April have to do with the rodeo?" Clay frowned. What the hell could what happened last night have to do with him and Mason joining the Professional Rodeo Cowboys Association?

Mason rolled his eyes. "Sometimes you don't use the brains the good lord gave you. I'm not talking about April. I'm talking about how you walked away with first prize while I ended up with a face full of dirt in under two seconds."

"Oh. But, so what? Everybody has a bad ride once in a while. I have."

"I seem to have more than my share, Clay, and you know it. I just don't know if I can make a living at it."

"We don't have to make a living at it. We can continue

to train horses for money and ride on the side."

Mason shook his head. "It won't be like it is now, Clay. To ride pro you are on the road constantly, pretty much year round. *You* can make it in that life. You are more than good enough. Everybody says so. I hear them talking after you come out of the chute. But me, I'm mediocre on a regular basis with a few good rides thrown in."

Clay opened his mouth to protest. It was true that Mason may not be good enough to be the best, but he would be able to rank within the top forty-five pro riders in the country in a few more years. He would at least be able to hold his own in the pros.

Mason cut off Clay, shaking his head. "It's your dream, Clay, and I wish it could be mine, too, but you're right, I am the worrier of the two of us. Sorry, but I think about things like paying the bills, a steady paycheck, and health insurance. I can't help it."

Clay couldn't argue that. Mason had grown up living hand to mouth at times after his daddy got injured and lost his job and his mama had to go to work. "So what will you do?"

Mason's eyes focused at a point over Clay's shoulder. "I'll tell you later. April's parents are coming out of the house. We better look like we just got here."

And they had better be convincing, that was for damn

sure, because this time, unlike the many other perfectly innocent nights they'd spent in April's bed, her daddy had good reason to shoot them. Clay kept that fact in mind as her father questioned them about how they'd ridden the night before and how his horses had performed.

They assured him they would feed and water the stock and turn them out, and then muck the stalls. With those promises made, the unsuspecting couple was off to church, leaving a still sleeping April and two very guilty cowboys behind.

Thinking about April still lying, soft and warm in her bed, Clay watched her parents' car turn onto the road and added one more thing to his personal to do list. He'd do all of his chores, but then he was heading directly home, locking himself in the bathroom, and taking care of this ache that one small taste of April had left him with.

Chapter Five

Mason sat beneath the baking hot noonday sun and watched the procession of graduates in their caps and gowns walk one by one up to the podium to receive their diplomas.

He'd gotten his that morning personally and privately in the principal's office. He wouldn't have even bothered coming to the ceremony now except that he was there to see April and Clay graduate. Their parents had the money to rent the stupid cap and gown, while Mason couldn't see clear to asking his parents to pay for something that seemed like such a waste. And he'd used half of his last paycheck for the rodeo entry fee and most of all his other pay went to help support his household, or pay for gas when they borrowed a vehicle to drive to competitions.

Clay, being Clay, had offered to pay for Mason's cap

and gown with part of his prize winnings, but Mason's pride wouldn't let him accept that. Besides, it would have been too late to place the order with the rental company anyway. The deadline for rentals was over a week ago.

The one unforeseen side benefit of being in the audience, instead of in the long line of graduating seniors waiting to receive their diploma, was that Mason had a clear and unobstructed view of Clinton as he made his way up to the podium. Apparently, one or the other of them had done some damage to Clinton's ribs the other night, judging by how gingerly he took the document from the principal and dodged to avoid the hearty one-armed hug the man had given to all the other graduates.

Mason had a dim recollection of kicking Clinton as the bastard curled in a ball on the ground, right about the time Clay had pulled him away. He allowed himself a small smile of satisfaction, while all the while realizing they both could have easily ended up in jail for assault, especially considering who Clinton's daddy was. But they hadn't.

Absently, Mason wondered what Clinton had told good old Dad about the bruises on his face. He probably said some gang had attacked and robbed him. Definitely not the truth, which was that he tried to take advantage of an innocent girl and paid the price for that mistake.

Meanwhile, April had been wearing long-sleeved t-shirts

in the heat to hide the bruises on her arms, and she'd had to cover the split in her lip with makeup. It didn't seem fair she had to bear the brunt of Clinton being an asshole.

Mason snapped to attention when he noticed it was April's turn to go up. Her cap balanced atop the expanse of tight, long, blond curls. Mason remembered the feel of that hair beneath his hands as he grabbed her head to kiss her that one night. The event had not been repeated in the days that followed. In fact, things had been a little strained between them, exactly as he'd feared.

Oh, she hadn't said anything to them to let them know how she felt. Maybe that was the problem. They didn't talk about it. Not one word. The three of them simply ignored that anything had happened at all. She was friendly, even while she took every opportunity to avoid being alone with them again, which is what led Mason to believe April regretted the whole thing. If it cost them the friendship, Mason would regret it, too.

He watched as she glided up to the podium, accepted the diploma and the kiss on the cheek from the principal and glided back. Once Clay went up, Mason was out of there. All the other kids would be meeting their families to go out to lunch. It was tradition. He didn't want anyone to take notice that not only had he not gone up, but he had no family there, either. He'd lied and said he didn't want to participate and convinced his parents it was silly for them to come since he wasn't in the procession. Besides, his mama had to work today, anyway.

Half the people probably assumed he didn't graduate at all, that he'd failed a class or something. Let them. What did he care? By the end of summer, when assholes like Clinton were off and killing time in college, he'd be gone.

Given that Mason was itching to get the hell away from this ceremony, it would be his luck that Clay would graduate almost dead last. They'd apparently lined up in height order and Clay was tall.

He watched Clay accept the diploma and then rose to leave, but by the time Mason got out of his row and through the throngs of people congratulating the graduates, April was in front of him, smiling. "You came."

Mason smiled down at her, her cheeks all flushed with excitement, her blue eyes twinkling, making his heart skip a beat. "Of course I did. I wouldn't have missed it for the world."

"Come to lunch with me and my parents."

This was exactly what he didn't want, a pity invite. "Nah, I got things I have to do at home."

"Okay. But meet me and Clay at the lake as soon as it gets dark. He says he has a graduation surprise for us."

Mason couldn't help but smile at her excitement. Maybe

the awkwardness of the last few days was finally over. "Okay. I'll be there."

"There are my parents. I have to go. See ya later!"

He nodded, counting the hours until dark and realizing as he watched her walk away from him that he was in very grave danger of having it real bad for that girl.

It wasn't hard to find Clay at the lake. He was camped out in the same spot they always met, and had been meeting, for five years now. Only this time, there was a blanket laid out on the ground, short, fat, lit candles tucked in the grass and two bottles of champagne sticking out of a red plastic cooler filled with ice.

Mason raised a brow. "Aw, Clay, how romantic. You shouldn't have."

Clay rolled his eyes. "It's for April. Well, we'll enjoy drinking the champagne, too, but the rest of this stuff..."

Was designed to get Clay into April's pants again, Mason finished Clay's sentence in is head.

Mason wasn't sure if this orchestrated seduction was pissing him off or a really good idea. As he tried to decide, April showed up, her smile lit by the candlelight as she took in the scene. "Wow. You guys did all this?"

Mason opened his mouth to protest that Clay did all this

alone when his friend jumped in and answered her. "Sure did. Have a seat, darlin'. Get comfortable."

Clay popped the first cork, poured them all a plastic cup full, and then held his cup high in the air. "To the three of us."

"The three of us," April echoed, holding up her own cup.

Those simple words had all new meaning after the other night. And the worst part was, repeating what they'd done together then was all he could think about tonight. Mason raised his cup silently and downed the contents in a single gulp.

Not sure if Clay had noticed his empty cup, or if Clay's goal was simply to get them all drunk, Mason allowed him to immediately pour him another anyway. Clay refilled April's cup and then his own, as well.

They continued to down the bubbly, chatting casually about nothing important, until the first bottle was empty and they were well into the second one.

After many more refills, April was holding up her cup and proposing the toast this time. "To never having to see that bastard Clinton's face in class again. And nice bruises, by the way. Good job, guys."

Mason paused, his champagne halfway to his lips. April was definitely feeling the effects of the alcohol. This was the first time she'd mentioned, or even alluded to what had happened that night with Clinton.

Clay accepted the compliment. "Thank you, ma'am." He downed the remaining contents of his cup and flopped back onto the blanket, the back of his head landing on April's thigh. "How can such a sissy drink make a person feel so drunk?"

April leaned back on her elbows, face tilted to gaze at the night sky. "I know why. I was so full from having lunch with my parents that I didn't have any dinner."

Clay laughed, rolling his head on April's leg to grin up at her. "Come to think of it, I didn't eat dinner, either. Hmm. That makes me feel better, at least. Thought I was turning into a lightweight."

Both of their voices were starting to show signs of intoxication.

Having skipped lunch, Mason had eaten a big dinner. Stretched out on the blanket and leaning back on his elbows, he realized he was definitely the most sober of the three by far. Not that he minded them being drunk, especially when April leaned heavily against his body.

It may have been shitty of him considering she was intoxicated, but when April slumped down and laid her head on his chest, then ran her hand absently up and down his stomach, he didn't object. Far from it. Instead, he leaned down and gently kissed the top of her hair.

51

She tilted her head up, gazed into his eyes and then touched her lips ever so softy to his before lowering her head again to rest against him. Which was when her hand strayed lower, down over the zipper in his jeans, to settle on his growing erection.

Mason's heart rate sped up. She would definitely feel it through his thin cotton shirt as clearly as she must feel the outline of his hard-on below.

Almost afraid to breathe and scare her away from touching him, he didn't move a muscle. He watched with rapt fascination as her delicate fingers fumbled slightly as she tried to undo the single button one-handed. He wanted to help her by stripping off the damn restrictive jeans, but he didn't. Finally successful with the button, she lowered the zipper with a rasp of metal that sounded much too loud to him in the darkness.

Clay heard it, too, and turned his head to look. When he saw April in the midst of freeing Mason's cock from his boxer briefs, he groaned. Sitting up on his knees, Clay unbuttoned April's khaki shorts, slid them down her legs, over her feet and flip flops, and laid them on the far corner of the blanket.

Mason realized Clay had pulled her panties off along with the shorts. April made no move to stop him. Mason didn't either as he greedily gazed down at April, naked from the waist down.

As April's hand began to stroke up and down Mason's bare length, he was moderately aware through his haze of pleasure of Clay getting undressed.

At any other time, Mason would have thought that Clay stripping off his jeans and underwear out in the open like this was a really bad idea. They should both be worried about so many things. What if her parents showed up here for some reason? What would April think about them moving so fast? Were they pushing her? Those were all the things Mason would have thought at any other time besides now, the exact moment that April leaned over and gently ran the tip of her tongue over the head of his nearly painful erection.

His eyes drifting closed, Mason drew in a sharp breath at the sensation. Then April slid the entire length of him into the hot wetness of her mouth and Mason couldn't hold himself up any longer on his shaky elbows. He laid back, his hand going instinctively to cup the back of her head as it bobbed over him.

She groaned deep in her throat, the sound reverberating through his body. Mason opened his eyes to see Clay nestled up close behind her. Dropping his gaze down, Mason got a view of the head of Clay's cock slipping slowly between her thighs while his hand parted her lower lips.

April trembled against him and opened her legs further

for Clay even as she took Mason deeper, all the way to the back of her throat, before pulling back again and scraping her teeth agonizingly down his length. He worked to control himself, to not grip her head and thrust into her mouth the way he longed to thrust into her body.

When he heard Clay whisper, "God, April, you're so wet," Mason had to work to not come in her mouth right then and there.

Still holding Mason in her closed fist, April pulled her mouth away and began to roll toward Clay, as if to give him attention equal to what she'd given Mason.

Clay shook his head and rolled her back on her side. "No, darlin'. Finish off Mason. I'm good."

Mason watched Clay's fingers begin circling April's clit faster, while just the tip of Clay's cock dipped inside of her. Her eyes squeezed shut, April lowered her head over Mason once more and he could no longer see what Clay was doing.

They shouldn't take April's virginity while she was drunk. It just wouldn't be right. And from what he'd seen, Clay was one good hard thrust away from doing exactly that. Before he lost his wits totally from the feel of her mouth on him, Mason caught Clay's eye and shook his head.

Clay nodded and readjusted himself so he was now sliding his cock up and down the crevice of her ass. Mason watched Clay's brow furrow as he squeezed his eyes shut tight from the friction. That was all the thought Mason could spare, because April was now using both hands and her mouth and he was getting too close to losing it to think of Clay.

Small rhythmic cries came from April's throat as she got closer to coming herself. Her breath picked up. Her one hand gripped him tighter while the other squeezed his balls, which were already drawn up tight, ready for him to finish this.

As April rocked back against Clay, Mason was barely aware of anything except the tingling building inside him, until he heard Clay let out a large whoosh of breath and say, "Yes! Oh, god. April."

The action of her hands and mouth became harder as she groaned deep in her throat and rocked, her body shaking all over as she began to come. Clay's breath was so fast and loud, Mason knew he was close, too. Managing to finally open his tightly closed eyes, Mason watched in shocked awe as Clay slid halfway into April's ass and held himself there while throwing his head back and shouting his release.

That was it. Mason couldn't take anymore. One hand tangled in April's curls, he held her head still and shot everything he had into her mouth.

They lay there for he didn't know how long, no one saying a word. Finally, April rose, pulled off her shirt and bra, modesty no longer an issue now, and strode into the lake without a word.

Mason watched her go, then turned on Clay. "What the hell were you doing, Clay? She's a virgin, for god's sake!"

Defensively, Clay shot him a look. "And she still is." Then he ran a hand over his face and let out a breath. Glancing at the lake to make sure April couldn't hear him as she washed herself, Clay lowered his voice. "I know. You're right. I'm sorry. I didn't mean to do that. I was fixin' to come from just rubbing against her, but she was so wet, and I got so slickery…" Clay shook his head. "Before I knew it, the tip was inside her. I would've pulled out, but she pushed back against me. I swear it, Mason, she kept pushing and before I knew it I was sunk halfway inside her ass. Then, that was it, there was no way I could stop from coming."

Scowling at that excuse, Mason shook his head.

"I swear to you, Mason. I wouldn't lie, not to you, not about this."

Mason glanced at the lake quickly to make sure she was still occupied. "You're trying to tell me she wanted that? Girls don't like doing that, Clay."

"That may be true for some, but not for her. You felt her as well as I did. She came harder this time than the last. And damn, Mason. I felt every squeeze of it inside her." Clay blew out a long slow breath over the memory. "And hey, I'm not bitching at you about coming in her mouth, am I? Girls aren't supposed to like that either, but you did it."

Mason sighed, guilty over coming in her mouth and hating himself for feeling jealous he and Clay's positions hadn't been reversed so he could have felt April come around his cock instead. How could doing something that felt so good make a person feel so bad afterwards? "Shit, Clay. This whole thing is getting way out of hand."

"So what do you suggest we do about it? 'Cause I have to tell you, I'm not willing to go back to being just friends after what's happened. Are you?"

Mason shook his head. "No, but it doesn't seem right, the three of us like this."

"What do we do then? Make her choose one of us? Is that really what you want?"

In the distance, April floated on her back under the moonlight. Her breasts two luminescent peaks above the water. After a long time, Mason whispered, "No."

"Then relax and enjoy this. No one is getting hurt."

Mason shook his head harder, not believing that was true. "It feels wrong."

Clay let out a breath of frustration. "We're not like that bastard Clinton, taking advantage of an innocent girl against her will. She cares about us. We both care about her. I always have, and lately…"

"Yeah, I know, Clay."

Clay didn't have to finish the sentence because Mason knew exactly what he was going to say. Lately, the caring was starting to feel like a whole lot more. And how the hell would that feel? Being in love with a girl you had to share with your best friend? He guessed it would be better than losing her to him completely.

April got out of the lake and walked back to them, dripping water. Suddenly, Mason realized how silly he felt. Him with his jeans still wide open. Clay, also lying on the blanket, naked from the waist down, except for his socks. Mason zipped and buttoned up his pants, glad no one had stumbled upon the scene.

April dressed again in the dark quickly. "Um. I gotta get to sleep." After that short goodbye, she left. Mason watched her speed away while Clay jumped up to get dressed himself. "We should walk her home."

Normally, they would have. Tonight, Mason shook his head. She'd be safe enough. The lake was on her daddy's property and her farmhouse and barns were barely a quarter mile down the private road.

"I don't think she wants the company, Clay." Mason sighed. "Have you noticed how she never wants to talk about it? About what happened with us."

"Girls are more uptight about sex and stuff than we guys are, I guess." Clay shrugged and with one last glance in the direction where April had disappeared, he apparently gave up on the idea of trying to walk her home. He flopped back onto the blanket, reached into the cooler and pulled out the last of the champagne. After taking a slug right out of the bottle, he handed it over to Mason, who took it gladly and guzzled a big gulp, regretting it when the bubbles slid painfully down his constricted throat.

Clay lay back and gazed at the sky. "I gotta tell ya', Mason. That was the most amazing thing I've ever felt in my life."

Mason felt his gut twist with need as he remembered peering past April's head to see Clay in her ass. Was he sick in the head that seeing that had made him come immediately? Although, he was eighteen. He could just about come if the wind blew hard enough. "Where do you reckon this thing between the three of us is gonna go?"

"I know where I hope it goes. I want her, Mason. Every inch of her. I want it all and I don't even care if I have to share her to get it. You're my best friend, and if sharing her is the only way to keep both of you, then that's what I'll do. As fucked up as this is, I'm afraid I'd lose one or both of you if she chose one of us over the other."

Clay grabbed the bottle Mason handed him back, took another mouthful and continued. "I'm afraid to even think about it. I don't think I could watch you with her every day and not be part of it. Could you?"

Mason didn't have to consider how he'd feel because he'd thought about it a lot lately. "If I was still here, no, I couldn't handle it."

Clay sat up and frowned. "What do you mean, if you were still here? Where the hell are you going?"

He'd avoided telling his friends long enough. Mason had been totally one hundred percent certain he knew what he wanted—until tonight, that was—and that sudden uncertainty scared the hell out of him. Time to start making plans before he did something stupid, like changing his mind. "I'm enlisting in the Army."

"Does this have to do with that idea of yours that you're not good enough to ride pro? Because that is just bull…"

"No, Clay. It's more than that. It's something I've been considering for a while now."

Clay's face fell. "You haven't done it yet, have you?"

"No. I figure I'll wait a bit and enjoy the summer." Mason couldn't lie to himself. He was also holding off so he could have more time enjoying April before he left her alone with Clay, knowing chances were good that Clay would make his big move on her once he left. They would be a couple, and he would be out.

Starting to feel depressed, Mason stood up and began packing things up, blowing out candles, gathering the used cups. Clay rose, shook out the blanket and began folding it. "I think you should be the one to do it first."

Mason glanced around, trying to see in the dark if they'd left anything. "Do what first?"

"Have her. You know. Take her virginity."

Mason stood dead still and stared at him. "What?"

"I mean, so far we've been sharing her just fine, but that particular event is a one shot deal. It can only be one of us and I think it should be you."

Mason swallowed, growing hard again at the thought while at the same time feeling how wrong it was to be discussing her like this. "Who says it's going to happen at all? That's up to her." But damn, he wanted it to happen.

"Yeah, of course it will be up to her when it happens, but it's gonna happen. It's only a matter of time. You know it and I know it after all the stuff that's already gone on just the two times we've been together."

He knew why Clay was making the gesture. It was his way of making up for the fact that the moment Mason hit boot camp, he'd very happily have April all to himself. Though Mason still had doubts the big "it" would happen. Yeah, she'd initiated anything that had gone on between them both times, but the first incident was when she was upset over Clinton and this time she was drunk. Then, she always drew back as if she regretted it afterwards, like tonight, when she went running away.

Still feeling like garbage for bargaining over April's virginity, Mason glanced at Clay. "I don't want to talk about this anymore because it makes me feel like an absolute shit."

"I'd rather discuss it now than wait until we're right in the middle of it, wouldn't you?"

Mason sighed. Clay could be like a bulldog with a bone when he set his mind to it. "If it will shut you up, okay, I agree. *If* it comes to that, I'll do it."

He hated the fact that he was rock hard and his palms were starting to sweat from just thinking about it.

Clay slapped an arm around Mason's back. "Good. Now come on. I'm sure the alcohol was flowing at rich boy's graduation party tonight and I don't trust Clinton to not try and take his mad at us out on April. Let's take a peek in her window and make sure she made it to bed safe. Then, I need to go home and sleep off this damned champagne."

That was Clay, always making sure everyone else was taken care of before thinking about himself. The worst part was that Mason couldn't even be jealous that Clay would get April in the end. When it came to choosing the best guy for April, Mason couldn't think of a better one than Clay. Considering Mason was about to willingly leave her, most likely to be shipped halfway around the world to a war zone, that included himself.

Even given that, he had to admit that while he was far away it would sure have been nice knowing April was his girl, waiting for him back home. How selfish was that?

And while he was feeling selfish, he might as well go all the way, so until he left, Mason would take anything April was willing to give. The heartbreak when he left in the end would suck beyond measure, but the memories they made together would have to be enough to last him a lifetime. He'd leave knowing she was in Clay's good hands and for that, Mason would have to force himself to be grateful.

Chapter Six

Clay watched April come out of the house, see him and Mason in the ring with the horse, and turn around again. *Shit.* Mason had guessed it right. April had avoided being alone with them after the first time they were all together, and she was doing the same thing again now.

"You were right. Things are messed up again with her."

Mason followed where Clay was looking and pressed his lips together. "Yeah, I know."

Resolved, Clay handed the lead rope to Mason. "I'm going to talk to her."

Mason looked doubtful. "You sure you want to do that?"

Clay nodded.

"Do you want me to come?"

Remembering how he had been the one who slid off her

shorts and underwear, before sliding into her, Clay shook his head. "Nah. I'm the one that did what I did. I think I need to talk to her alone." He hesitated. "You okay with that?"

Mason raised a brow. "You're asking my permission to talk to April?"

Clay laughed sadly. "Yeah, I know. That's messed up, huh? But…"

"Things are a little messed up right now all around," Mason finished his thought.

"Yeah, they are." Especially if April was going to avoid them, possibly because of something Clay had done. He needed to straighten it out. And even though he and Mason shared a whole hell of a lot, especially lately, this he had to handle alone.

Mason tilted his head toward the house. "Go on. I'll put the horse away and start on the afternoon chores."

Clay nodded his thanks and headed for the house. Luckily April's parents were away at a horse sale so they could safely talk about this inside without fear of being heard. He let himself in the back door quietly, feeling how much cooler the well-shaded house felt than standing in the sun out in the ring. The sounds of a television led him to the family room, where April lay back on the seat cushion with her feet kicked up and hanging over the arm of the sofa.

"Hey."

65

She startled at his voice, then recovered quickly and focused her eyes back on the television. Figuring he was in for a long haul since she wouldn't even look at him, he sat down right next to her so that the top of her head touched his thigh.

He played with one of her curls. "I want to talk about last night."

He sensed her body stiffen. "I don't."

"Why not?"

"There's nothing to talk about."

"I think there is. Mason thinks you're avoiding us because you regret what we all did together."

She became very still, barely breathing for a moment. "And what do you think?"

"I didn't agree with him until I saw you take one look at me in the ring then hightail it back inside. Now I'm starting to wonder if I pushed you too far last night. And if I did, I'm sorry. Real sorry."

He tipped her chin up so she had to look at him upside down. "Did I go too far?"

She shook her head and he felt a weight lift, until she pulled her chin away and looked anywhere but at him.

"You sure, darlin'? You can tell me. I know sometimes *that*, you know, what I did at the end, can hurt a girl."

April sat up abruptly and looked away. "Can we *please*

talk about something else?"

Clay silently mouthed a curse. "I did hurt you."

"No, you didn't."

He wished she would at least look at him. He continued, not believing her answer. "When you pushed back against me, I figured you liked it or I would have stopped."

April buried her reddened face in her hands. "Clay, please. Can't we drop this?"

He grabbed her wrist gently and pulled the hand closest to him away from her face. "No. I can't. Not until you tell me if I hurt you. I wanted to make you feel good. I would never hurt you on purpose."

She took a deep breath before finally answering him. "It did feel good. Okay? In the very beginning, when you were just kind of there, rubbing and pushing against me, it was incredible. That's why I pushed back. But then, when you were first inside, it did hurt a little bit. I almost asked you to stop, but you sounded like it felt so good, I didn't."

He felt horrible. "Dammit, April, don't let me ever do anything that hurts you, I don't care how good it feels for me. Tell me next time, okay?" Clay wanted this point made very clear because he anticipated many more nights with April and he really wanted there to be a next time.

Finally turning toward him, she really looked at him for the first time since he'd arrived. She put one finger across his lips. "Let me finish. I was going to say that the other thing you were doing to me with your hand was so amazing that the hurt went away. And then when I started to…you know…it all felt good. *Really* good."

Clay smiled at how she blushed and couldn't say the words because of her embarrassment. Stroking her face with one finger, he shook his head in wonder. "You are amazing. And next time, I'll be prepared so it won't hurt you at all. I promise."

April's face turned vivid red right before she threw her hands up to cover it again. "Clay! Just because I liked doing it doesn't mean I want to talk about it!"

He grinned. "Okay, okay. No more talking about it, but I still don't understand. If you're okay with what happened, then what's with the hiding in the house and avoiding Mason and me?"

She shook her head and moved away.

He grabbed her arm and kept her near him. "What? Tell me."

April turned and faced away from him. Clay forced her to turn back to him and found tears in her eyes. "April. What is it? Tell me."

Shaking her head again, she freed herself from his grasp, stood and ran out of the room, leaving Clay alone and more confused than before. Blowing out a loud breath of frustration, he left April alone in the house.

Clay caught up with Mason outside the hayshed.

"So?" he asked when he saw Clay.

Clay let out a short laugh. "So, things are about as clear as mud now."

Mason dropped the bale of hay on the ground and propped one boot on it, adjusting the brim of his hat. "What happened?"

"I asked her if it was what I'd done to her last night that had her hiding from us and she said no. Then when I asked her what *was* wrong, you know if it wasn't that, she got all teary and ran out of the room."

"She was crying? Shit." Mason sighed. "So what do we do?"

Clay shrugged. "Hell if I know. I guess we give her some space and she'll come around just like she did last time." He laughed and looked at Mason sadly. "How long did it take her last time?"

Mason glanced at the house. "Three long days."

Clay followed Mason's gaze and let out a long slow breath. "One down, two to go."

Three days passed and April still talked to them only when she had to, and then, only about things that were inconsequential. Clay had great hopes for this summer but things were not looking too good at the moment. Although some of the stuff that had happened with April already was beyond his wildest dreams, the tension between them now just plain sucked.

Lying in his bed in the dark, Clay ran over and over their last real conversation when she'd run out of the room crying. What the hell was with girls? If Mason was pissed about something, he'd outright tell Clay what it was. Not avoid him for days on end so he had to guess. Things had been so much simpler when April was just one of the guys.

Then Clay remembered her taste, the feel of her beneath his hands, the sensations of being inside her, and he reconsidered that opinion. Things had been simpler, but not nearly as good, that was, until she freaked out and started to avoid them both.

Angry now that she wouldn't open up to him, one of her best friends, Clay swung his bare feet from the bed and stood. He'd had enough. Throwing on whatever clean clothes his hands found first in his drawers, Clay was dressed and sneaking out of the house in about two minutes.

It was barely a ten-minute walk to April's farm. The night being cooler than the past few had been, Clay was able to travel at a fairly brisk pace and still arrive hardly having broken a sweat.

The room was dark, the window open. Clay's heartbeat picked up speed just from seeing it and knowing she lay right inside. Hopping up onto the sill, he swung in and stopped dead as April squeaked with surprise. Her hand that had been between her splayed, naked thighs grabbed the sheet to cover her nakedness.

Clay stood, shocked, speechless, and hard enough to hammer nails from what he'd seen. The image was seared into his brain—April, lying back on the bed, legs spread wide, her fingers frantically working between them.

"Dammit, Clay! What the hell? Get out of here!"

Catching barely enough breath to speak, Clay took one step forward. "Darlin', you're gonna have to physically throw me out of that window because after seeing that, there is no way I can leave under my own steam."

She groaned and covered her face with the sheet balled in her hands. "Please, go away."

If she really had wanted him to leave, he would. But he knew that wasn't the case. At the moment, she was pretty mortified at being caught, but that was all. Clay knew exactly how she felt, but if she had any idea how often he'd masturbated in the last week, she'd know she had nothing to be ashamed of.

Clay perched on the edge of the mattress and pulled her into his arms. She didn't exactly fall into him, but she didn't fight him. "April, darlin', there's nothing for you to be embarrassed of. Believe me. Now, when my mama walked in on me a few years back when I was occupied doing the same thing, *that* was embarrassing."

April uncovered her face and looked at him wide-eyed. "She did? Really?"

Clay laughed. "Oh, yeah."

"What'd she do?"

"Turned right around and never brought it up again. Although, my papa did visit me that next day to have 'the talk'." Clay squeezed her harder. "So you see, you should be happy. It could have been a hell of a lot worse. It's only me seeing you. That's nothing."

In the soft light of the nightlight, he watched April roll her eyes. "I still wish you would knock or something."

He laughed. "Knock? At the window?"

"Yeah!"

Clay ran one hand up and down her back. "Okay. Next time I'll knock. So, uh..." He'd come here to talk, but after seeing what he'd seen, he now had other ideas. "You want any, um, help with what you were doing?"

She covered her face again. He reached up and pulled her hands away, grinning at how damn cute and shy she was, all while being sexy as hell.

Finally making eye contact, she spoke. "It doesn't work

for me."

Clay raised a brow. "What do you mean?"

April hesitated. "I try, sometimes for a long time, but nothing happens. Not like when you do it."

He drew in a deep breath as his stomach twisted with want. That was probably the hottest thing she'd ever said to him. She couldn't get off on her own without him and that really, really turned him on.

Clay swallowed, but his voice still sounded raspy to his own ears. "Good thing I showed up then."

Then a thought hit him, a wonderful, tantalizing thought. Was it possible April had never had an orgasm before him? As his heart pounded like it was trying to get out of his chest, Clay asked, "That first night we were all together. Was that the first time that you ever…you know?"

She nodded.

Ready to come right then and there just from the conversation, he lowered his head and she didn't pull away, but instead leaned in and met his lips. Clay pushed aside the guilty feeling that he was undercutting Mason. Loyalty and friendship were important, but April was soft, warm and wanting in his arms, and that was all he could think about.

Her soft kiss became more when he plunged his tongue inside to meet hers. When his hand strayed down between her thighs and found her clit already swollen, he groaned.

She'd obviously worked it hard even though she couldn't get herself over the edge.

Sliding one finger inside her, he felt the ready slickness there. She was making sexy little sounds that nearly did him in as he touched her. It would be so tempting to slide himself inside her and forget all about Mason and the deal they'd made.

Making her pleasure his priority, Clay found and stroked the spot inside of her that he'd read about in a men's magazine, knowing he was doing it right when she whimpered louder in her throat. Maybe he was showing off, trying to prove to her that he could not only get her off, but he knew more than one way to do it, too. He worked her G-spot with two fingers until he felt her muscles bearing down. Only then did he pay attention to her swollen clit.

Her whole body trembled and he knew she'd come soon, just from his touch. That thought made him really hot.

She exploded around him and Clay knew he better do something to relieve himself and fast before he whipped his dick out and took her completely.

When her body began to calm, he pulled away.

April let out a small sound of protest when he stopped touching her, her hips following his hand up when he took it away. He grinned as he stood. "Don't worry, darlin'. I'm coming back to you in just a sec."

She watched through heavily lidded eyes as he stripped off his boots, jeans and t-shirt and then finally, his boxers. Yeah, it was stupid being naked in her room. If her parents came down the hall for any reason, he'd have about two seconds to gather everything up and jump out the window, and even then, he'd be outside in the yard butt ass naked. At the moment, Clay didn't care. He did, however, pile his clothes beneath the window, just in case. Better safe than sorry.

Her eyes were wide as she watched him crawl onto the bed next to her, led by the pole jutting straight out from his body that pointed to her like a homing device.

Clay stretched out next to her, his erection pointing at the ceiling now. It felt really good to be lying naked next to her. A little too good. He could get used to this real easy. Making love to her right now would feel even better.

He bent his knees and slid further down on the bed so there was space between his head and the headboard. "Get on top of me, darlin'?"

Clay had made it a question, not an order, but she did as asked and crawled on top, facing him. Her hair hung down around her flushed face making her look like an angel. At the same time, her sweet and tempting pussy hovered much too close to his ready cock.

Clay reached up and kissed her, just a quick peck before

he did something he might regret later. "Now spin around so you're facing my feet."

April raised a brow but again did as he asked. He loved how she trusted him.

His hands on her hips guided her backwards until she was lined up perfectly, right where he needed her to be. Her pussy hovered above his head, his cock aligned with her mouth. She stiffened a bit over him, having never been in this position before he was fairly certain.

"Relax, darlin'." His kissed one pale cheek, then the other, and then Clay set to proving all over again just how well he, and only he, could make her come.

Latching his mouth onto her, he zeroed in on her clit and scraped it gently with his teeth, before soothing it again with his tongue. He felt the shiver run through her at that.

His long groan of deep satisfaction when she slid her mouth down over his erection came out muffled. The sound must have vibrated through her in a good way, because she twitched above him and moaned.

He loved the taste of her, the feel of her over him, the way she trembled in his arms as her muscles clenched when she got close to coming. Especially, he loved how he knew exactly how to touch her to make her come so easily.

With his tongue sliding in and out of the one place he desperately wanted to go but hadn't, Clay wet one finger and began circling the place he had already been and really hoped to be again. April stilled and her body briefly clenched tightly against his probing.

Clay's mouth zeroed back in on her clit as he continued plying her with his wet finger until her body finally opened, slowly accepting him, welcoming him inside. It was her trigger, a guaranteed hot button, something Clay had discovered that very first time the three of them had been together. He'd never told Mason what he'd done to finally push her over the edge that first night. It just didn't seem right to discuss details about her like that. Now, it was Clay and April's little secret, something he knew about her that no one else knew. He had to share so much already, he wanted something just for himself.

He had just worked the tip of one finger inside her when she came, hard and fast, pulsing over him violently. Writhing above him, April bore down, her mouth and hand tightening over his cock, speeding her motions as she came, chasing all thought except for the feel of her out of Clay's head. It was almost enough to make him follow right behind her, but not quite.

As her spasms died down, the movements of her mouth and hand on him slowed and he nearly cried with frustration. "Keep going, darlin'. Please, I'm so close."

April readjusted her position over him, then Clay felt her

tiny, wet finger slide back, behind his balls, to begin probing him. His body involuntarily clenched tight against the invasion.

Clay let out a shuddering breath, silently chanting the word "relax" in his brain. He'd read about this, too. The male G-spot, guaranteed to make any man come if manipulated correctly, *if* he could get his body to let her inside. Her touching him like that was a little bit frightening and very, very intriguing at the same time.

She gathered more spit on her finger and circled him, teasing his hole. She'd abandoned his cock for the moment but he was too fascinated with what she was doing, what he was feeling, to care.

Between the slickness of her saliva and her patient probing, Clay felt it happening, his body finally opening for her, just like hers always did for him. The tightness eased just enough and she slid part of the way inside. He squeezed his eyes shut and threw his head back against the mattress, trying not to clench up as she pushed inside him. She moved gently, slowly. He raised his hips off the mattress slightly to give her more access as she worked just the tip of her finger in and out. April took him inside her mouth again while moving her finger faster.

Clay took a shuddering breath as what he suspected would be unbelievable pleasure hovered just out of his reach.

"A little deeper, darlin'."

Since his cock was already deep in her throat, she figured out he meant her finger and pushed further inside. She hit right where he needed her to and his body jolted. He felt the familiar tingle inside his balls and trembled as he came harder than ever, pulsing inside her mouth, muffling his cries by burying his face against her thigh.

Her mouth milked him as her finger continued stroking until the intensity of it all turned from pleasure to pain and he had to squirm to pull out of her mouth.

As breathless as Clay, April shakily crawled off him, spun around and landed heavily on the bed. He rolled on his side, flopped one arm over her and blew out a long breath. "Wow."

April let out a breath of her own. "Yeah."

Then right before his eyes, he watched her shut down, like a door closing between them. They'd just shared something pretty amazing and he wanted to talk about it. Why didn't she?

"April, don't."

"Don't what?" Her voice was soft.

"Don't close me out. Please. You do it every time we're together. Why?"

She was silent for so long he thought she wouldn't answer. "Do you ever think about the future?"

Hmm. Was this a radical change of subject or did this have something to do with the two of them? "Sure, I do. I want to go pro and ride as long as I'm physically able, then retire and buy a horse farm with the money from my winnings."

"See. You have a whole plan mapped out for the future."

"You do, too. I thought you were enrolling in the community college this fall."

"So I can do what? Graduate and substitute teach for a few years until I get married and have babies of my own, just like my mother did?"

Clay imagined her married to him, having his babies. "You're mama's life looks pretty good to me."

She let out a sound of disagreement before saying, "I did something. Nobody knows. Not even my parents."

The suspense nearly killed Clay as he waited for her to finish her sentence. She finally did. "I applied to NYU. I got in. With a pretty decent scholarship, too."

Vainly hoping that there was another NYU somewhere in Oklahoma he hadn't heard about, Clay asked, "New York?"

She nodded.

"You're going?" Just because she'd gotten in didn't mean she'd actually go.

"Yes, I think so. I really want to. I want to live life

before I settle down."

Okay, he could handle that. Four years. She'd come home for holidays and summer break. He'd visit her in New York when the circuit took him out east. Then, she'd come back for good and settle down here.

She continued talking while Clay's brain worked.

"But that's the problem. Every time we're together—you, me, and Mason—I'm afraid I won't go. That I won't want to leave you both and I'll stay here." Her hand found his and she laced their fingers together. "I want you, Clay."

He swallowed hard at that revelation. "Good, because I want you, more than anything."

She continued softly. "But, I want Mason, too. And that's a problem."

Clay shut his eyes for a second and absorbed her confirmation of what he already knew but had managed to push aside over the past hour.

The mention of Mason's name also brought back the guilt. How the hell was he going to explain this night to Mason? But at least she was talking about things, which was more than she'd done for the past week. He'd deal with Mason later.

He played with her hand in his. "So that's what's been bothering you? I know you want Mason too. I can handle it. It's okay."

She spun on him. "No it's not okay, Clay. What kind of whore am I that I want you both?"

"You are not a whore!" But besides that, he didn't have an answer for her. This triangle of theirs was as new and weird for him as it was for her, and, Clay was sure, for Mason, too.

She hesitated and he knew there was more coming. "People choose one person to fall in love with, Clay. One person to marry and be with for the rest of their lives. Not two. What kind of person am I that I love you both?"

Heart in his throat, Clay touched her face. He noticed his hand trembled. Hearing a woman loved you could do that to a man, he guessed. Saying it back could shake a guy up, too. Clay's voice sounded a bit emotional when he said, "You're a person with the biggest most loving heart of anyone I know. That's why I love you."

He slid his arm beneath her head and leaned in, kissing her deeply. Clay imagined he could taste himself on her tongue, but it didn't matter. April was in his arms and she loved him. That was all that mattered. Yeah, she loved Mason too, but he'd just have to deal with that.

She pulled back. "Don't tell Mason about college. It's something I have to tell him myself. Okay?"

He nodded and lowered his mouth to hers again. Then he slid lower as his tongue trailed down her throat to nibble at the tip of one breast. Her back arched at his touch, pressing her body closer against him.

Clay decided to be selfish and keep her to himself for a little bit longer tonight. He'd share her again, for as long as that was what she wanted, but for now, he wanted to pretend the woman he loved was all his.

Chapter Seven

Mason stood watching Clay in the saddle atop one of the new horses in the ring. He was good. A natural. He moved with the horse's motion rather than fighting it, his timing was perfect, almost as if he could read the animal's mind and sense what he would do next. Watching him reaffirmed to Mason that his decision was the correct one.

"Hey."

April's soft voice behind him was as welcome as a cool rain on a hot summer night. Mason turned, and when he saw her shy smile, he returned it with a warm one of his own. They hadn't really spoken since the night at the lake, but she was here now and that was all that mattered.

"Hey, baby." Glancing at the house to make sure no one was coming, Mason ran one hand down her arm, enjoying even this small contact. "I've missed you."

Her eyes lowered at first, she finally raised them to meet his. "I've missed you too, Mason."

That knowledge made him smile more broadly. "I'm glad."

"Mason. I kind of need to talk to you about something."

That wiped the grin right off his face. He swallowed. "Um. Okay. When?"

"Tonight, after my parents go to sleep. My room."

Mason nodded and then she turned and left. He was still frozen when Clay swung off the horse and came to stand next to him. "What did she want?"

He finally broke his gaze from watching her walk away. "She says she needs to talk to me. Tonight."

Clay glanced at the house. "Did she say why?"

"No. But I didn't ask, either. I was afraid to." Mason let out a short laugh at himself.

"Afraid of what?"

"That's she's going to tell me she's made a decision between the two of us. That she's chosen you."

"Why would you think that?" Clay was acting strangely, speaking quieter than usual, almost carefully.

"Because she didn't ask you to come to her room tonight." Mason squinted against the sun's glare at Clay. "Did she?"

Clay shook his head. "No."

Mason let out a long slow breath. "Shit."

The hours between afternoon chores and nightfall seemed to fly, the one time that Mason wished they would drag. Where normally he'd want to see April, instead, tonight, he dreaded it and what she would tell him with every fiber of his being.

But the June sun had set, and Mason knew April's parents would be in bed sleeping by nine, as usual. He had no excuse, so he told his parents he was going to Clay's house, that he might spend the night there, and then he headed down the road to April's farm.

If she dumped him, he could always come home again and say he couldn't sleep at Clay's and wanted his own bed. If she didn't (doubtful, but Mason could hope) he could spend a long, blissful night in her bed, alone with her. That would be really nice. He'd never done that before, been there alone with her, even when the three of them had been only friends.

The road had never seemed so short or the distance to her windowsill so high as he dragged the toe of his boot through the dirt and dreaded coming face to face with her.

Finally, he couldn't put it off any longer. He jumped up

and easily pulled his weight over the sill. Today, April didn't lie in the bed in her darkened room, but instead, sat in a chair by the window, waiting for him. He didn't like the change.

"Hi."

"Hi," she returned.

Mason walked to the bed and sat on the edge facing her. Feet planted firmly on the ground, he rested his forearms on his knees and leaned forward. As ready as he'd ever be, he said, "Alright. Go ahead."

April laughed nervously. "You're acting like you're in the principal's office or something."

He sat up straighter and tried to look casual as he waited for her to crush him. "Sorry."

She shook her head and let out a short laugh. "It's okay. Um, anyway, I have something to tell you."

Mason swallowed hard and stared at a point just past her head. "Okay."

"I, uh, I'm going to college in New York in the fall. I didn't tell anyone when I applied, not even my parents. I wasn't even sure I'd get in. But I did, with a scholarship, and I'm going."

Mason's gaze swung to her. "That's it? That's what you had to tell me?"

She nodded. "Yeah."

"Nothing else?"

"No."

Laughing, he stood, lifted her into his arms and swung her around. "That's great! I am very happy for you."

April laughed, too, hanging on to his shoulders tightly. "Yeah, I can see that."

Finally, regretfully, he put her down, but didn't let her go. Mason leaned down and brushed his lips across hers in what he told himself was a congratulatory kiss.

He had come in contact with her bare flesh when he'd picked her up in that t-shirt she slept in. Craving more, he slid his hands up beneath the bottom of the t-shirt, up over her panties, and felt the warm skin as his hands circled her waist. Touching her was starting to get to him now that he knew she wasn't cutting him loose to be with Clay exclusively.

Mason sat in the chair and pulled her into his lap. She came to him willingly, so much smaller than him that she could curl right up in his lap with her head nestled against his chest and her ass nestled against something lower.

He kissed her again, letting his tongue slide against hers. His hands strayed higher on her thighs, longing to dip inside her and see if she wanted him as much as he wanted her.

But there was something he had to tell her first, before he let his hands go any further.

"While we're telling things, I've got something to tell

you, too. I've made a decision. I'm going to enlist in the Army at the end of the summer."

April stiffened and frowned. "But you were going to ride with Clay."

"I'm not as good as he is and you know it. I'd have a mediocre career in his shadow. I don't want that."

"But the Army. Mason, we're in a war. You could get killed."

He let out a laugh. "I could get crippled or killed just as easily in the rodeo as in the Army. You know that."

Frowning again, she struggled to get off his lap. "I don't want you to go."

"You're going away to college."

She huffed out an angry breath. "That's totally different!"

Mason shook his head, his voice calm and steady, not reflecting what he felt inside at all. "No, not really. The fact is, you can secretly apply months ago to a college halfway across the country and not tell me you're going 'til now, but I decide a few days ago I'm going to join the Army and tell you about it and you're mad at me. Just like how you were mad at Clay and me for going to Elk City instead of the prom, and look where that got you."

He regretted the words the minute they left his mouth. The look on her face at what he'd said was as horrified as if he had slapped her. In the dim light, Mason could see the tears glistening in her eyes.

"Look, I'm sorry." He needed her to support him in his decision, to understand why he'd had to make it. She obviously didn't. Mason let out a breath of frustration. "I'm gonna go." *Before I make things worse*, he added silently.

With one glance back, he swung over the sill and slid to the ground. He strode as fast as he could away from her before he did something stupid, and changed his mind and went back. She was mad and upset and there was nothing he could say or do to make things better. Hell, he was pretty mad and upset himself. They'd both have to get over it in their own time.

He would. No way he could stay mad at her, then, he'd apologize again and think of a way to make it up to her. If she let him.

Mason allowed himself one indulgence and stopped by the lake on his way home. He stared at the water shimmering beneath the moonlight, remembering their time together there, when he heard footsteps running.

He turned in time to catch an armful of crying angry woman. April beat at him with her fists and then collapsed against his chest, sobbing. "I hate you for joining the Army and going away."

"Shhh. It's okay." Mason held her tightly against him.

Her face crushed against his chest, he could hardly hear her. "No, it's not. You're going to go and get yourself killed."

Not if he had anything to say about it, he wouldn't. Mason rubbed her back, realizing she'd shoved her feet into flip flops and ran after him in nothing but the t-shirt she'd been wearing in her room.

Her sobs quieted, finally stopping until she whispered against his chest, "I love you."

Mason's breath caught in his chest at hearing that. As he lifted her up to kiss her, she wrapped her legs around his waist. His erection pressing against her panties, he groaned and plunged his tongue inside her mouth.

April moved against him, her breath catching in her throat each time her shift in weight rubbed the crotch of her panties against the bulge in his jeans. April getting herself off by rubbing against him was more than Mason could take. He wanted inside of her and now.

Mason walked them both to the water's edge and lowered her to the ground. He stripped off his clothes as quickly as he could as she, thankfully, did the same. He lifted her again. April naked before him in the moonlight was a dream come true, but April naked and in his arms in the water was almost more than he could bear.

Her legs were around him once more, but this time,

91

nothing separated them. Mason waded them into the pond, the cool water making her nipples hard against his chest as she clung to him. With his cock nestled between her legs, once they were chest deep in the water she was buoyant enough to move freely over him, rubbing against his tip.

He watched the rapt look on her face as, eyes closed, she worked his cock to sit just at her entrance. Mason drew in a deep breath and held it as she moved just the first inch of him in and out of herself. Then she did the one thing he'd been dreaming of for the past week and lowered her body over him.

April stared at him, wide-eyed, as her own weight slowly forced his whole length inside of her incredibly tight pussy, until he was hilt deep with her seated tightly against him. He didn't move, just held her as her eyes closed and he felt a shiver run through her.

His lids drifted shut as he felt both the cold of the water and the heat of April's body surround him. He supported her weight easily with his hands beneath the water, and it took only the slightest of movements on his part to raise and lower her over him.

It blew his mind to think he was the first man to do this to her. He had to be. They'd known her for years and besides the prom, she'd never spent any time with another guy, and she'd sworn nothing had happened that night with Clinton.

Mason had had sex with a woman before, so had Clay. They'd ridden in a rodeo out of state and stayed overnight. It was easy for a bronco rider, even an amateur, to get laid if he really wanted to. And he and Clay, tired of being virgins, had wanted to. When two girls approached them, flirting and showing way too much boob to be interested in anything besides fucking, they hadn't thought twice about it, except to run to the men's room and buy a half a dozen condoms, because who knew where those girls had been before them.

But that night had been nothing like this. This was April and she loved him. And as painful as he knew it was going to be later when he left for boot camp and she left for college, he loved her, too. He whispered the words against her ear now as he made love to her. Tears in her eyes, she looked at him, then kissed him again.

They took it slowly, partly because he didn't want to hurt her during her first time, mostly because he never wanted it to end. But every stroke inside of April had him falling more under her spell until his world narrowed to nothing except the sound of her breathing near his ear and the feel of her body covering his.

He reached between them with one hand and found the spot where their bodies joined, the place that caused her to start shaking, finally convulsing around him.

Mason felt himself reach the point of no return and

reality came crashing in around him. He yanked her up and off him as he started to come.

Not willing to put her down and too shaky to carry her up onto the grass, Mason stayed with her in the water afterwards, April still wrapped around him. When she kissed him, he kissed back, but his mind was reliving that final moment, calculating if he'd pulled out in time. Considering what they'd do if he hadn't. And since he was already ruining the perfect night by worrying, Mason added Clay's name to his list of things to stress over.

Letting them drift deeper toward the center of the pond, he let them bob, neck deep. "Can I tell you something?"

She nodded.

"I figured you were fixin' to dump me tonight."

April's brow furrowed. "Why would you think that?"

"You asked to talk to me, not Clay. I thought you'd decided you wanted only him and not me."

"Do you still think I would do that?"

"No." He laughed and then sobered when a thought hit him. "When are you going to tell Clay about New York?"

Her answer nearly sunk him. "I already did. Last night."

Stunned speechless, all he could do was think that perhaps he hadn't been her first after all.

Chapter Eight

"I had sex with April last night." Mason paused, and then added, "And, I know you were with her the night before."

Clay swallowed hard and waited for the axe to fall while Mason, jaw firmly set in a familiar expression that said he wasn't happy, stared off into the distance.

Finally, Mason turned to look at him. "I'm not sure I can do this anymore. This feeling inside me when I think of you being with her alone sucks, and I don't even know what, if anything, happened between you two the other night."

At that, Clay realized April hadn't told him what happened, just that they'd been together. Clay watched Mason rub his chest, as if to relieve a pain there. Picturing him with April last night and knowing for a fact what they had done, Clay understood a bit about how Mason was feeling.

"Would it be better if you did know what happened?" Clay offered.

Mason laughed bitterly. "I doubt it."

"Well, if it helps any, I swear to you, I didn't mean for anything to happen at all. I only went there to talk."

Mason laughed again. "Yeah, I know. So did I."

"So if you don't want to do this anymore, what do we do? Have her choose between us? Or does one of us bow out?"

Raising a brow, Mason looked at him. "You willing to bow out?"

There was absolutely no doubt in Clay's mind as to his answer to that question. "No. You?"

Mason shook his head. "No. Before last night, maybe I could have, but not now. She told me she loves me."

"Yeah, me, too."

Mason turned to look at him. "She told you she loves you?"

Clay laughed. "Yeah, but don't worry. It was in the same breath she told me she loves you, too."

"So we're both in the same boat here, it seems."

Clay nearly let it go, but just couldn't. He was too pissed Mason had gone all the way with her on his own, without him being there. "Yeah, except that you're going away."

Mason looked defensive. "So is she."

"She's going to New York. You're likely going to Iraq or hell, I don't know, Afghanistan, for all you know."

"So you're saying you're better for her than me, even though you'll be on the road all the time, risking breaking your neck and surrounded by hoards of women intent on fucking the star rodeo rider?"

Frowning, Clay took a step closer to Mason, about to protest the insinuation that he would ever cheat on April, when she was suddenly there behind them.

"Stop it! Both of you. Stop fighting."

Mason swore quietly beneath his breath.

"April." Clay took a step towards her.

She held one hand up. "No. Don't touch me. I'm mad at you both. Neither one of you is being fair to me. You're standing out here discussing me and who's better for me like it's your place to do so, without even caring what I want. If you're going to fight over me, then I won't be with either one of you."

"Now, hold up there, darlin'. Don't go being hasty." Clay risked it and took a step closer. The warning look she shot him froze him in place.

"You're right. It's not our place. So then tell us. What *do* you want us to do, April?" Mason always was the more logical of the two of them.

97

Her voice sounded quiet, desperate. "I don't want to have to choose between you."

Lips clamped tightly shut, Mason drew a deep breath in through his nose. Clay waited and finally, Mason said, "Okay."

Clay raised a brow in surprise. "Okay?"

"Okay. She doesn't have to choose. We continue as we have been, the three of us, until she goes to college and I go to boot camp. Then, after that, we'll see what happens." Mason finally cracked a wry smile. "Who knows? Maybe she'll find some college boy and dump us both."

April frowned. "Hey!"

"Kidding, baby. Kidding." Mason laughed for real this time. It was a good sound.

She screwed up her face, apparently not quite ready to forgive them yet. Walking away, she shot back at them over her shoulder, "I suppose I'll be seeing you both tonight in my room."

Or maybe she had forgiven them.

It wasn't exactly an engraved invite, but it was good enough for Clay. They both watched her walk away. Once she was back in the house, Clay turned to Mason. "You really okay with this?"

Mason stared into space for a second. "Yeah. I think I really am. It's kind of a relief to stop worrying about who she'd choose if we forced her to."

Clay let out a long slow breath, nearly vibrating at the thought of what April had said when she left. "So, tonight, huh?"

Mason nodded. "Yup. Seems like. And before tonight, you and I have something we need to do."

It was that statement that had led to the two of them borrowing Clay's mother's car and standing in the condom aisle of a convenience store three towns away where they hoped no one would know them.

Mason had picked up a small package but Clay shook his head. "Better get the big box."

With a raised brow, he picked up the large one marked "value pack" instead while Clay reached past him and grabbed a bottle of personal lubricant off the shelf. "This too."

Clay had watched Mason swallow as his eyes opened wider. "Okay. Is that it?"

Nodding, Clay had taken a few bills out of his wallet. "Yeah. Let's pay and get the hell out of here."

And now Clay stood with Mason beneath April's window, a not-so-small brown paper bag containing a box of three-dozen condoms and a bottle of lube in hand.

"Why the hell am I nervous?" Clay hissed to Mason.

"Because this is the first time we've actually planned it. Before, it just kind of happened."

Deciding the only way to get over the nerves was to get on with it, Clay grabbed the windowsill. "Come on."

Once inside, Clay's eyes searched the dark room. He saw April lying on the bed, but not in an over-sized t-shirt like she usually wore. It appeared she had done a bit of shopping of her own. She was laid out before them like a centerfold. Blond hair splayed on the pillow, breasts spilling from two small pyramids of white lace, with another matching lace triangle between her legs.

Clay swallowed hard, damn glad they'd come with provisions, because looking at her now, laid out like a sexual buffet, there was no way they weren't going to take advantage of every inch of her.

Mason stood next to him, still as a statue. "Where do we start?"

Clay laughed, knowing exactly where he wanted to start. He opened the bag, dumped the contents on the end of the bed, grabbed April's feet, and pulled her to the edge of the mattress as she squealed.

"Clay!"

"Mmm. You can't look like this and expect to not be ravaged by the two cowboys you invited to your bedroom after dark, darlin'."

She giggled as he planted her feet on his chest and leaned down to nibble on one bare toe. The view looking down her long, lean legs to that tempting triangle was pretty damn nice. Clay decided to take a closer look and kneeled at the end of the bed, eyelevel with his heart's desire.

He discovered the panties were a thong. Nothing but a string on each hip and one between her ass cheeks held that piece of lace on her enticing body. Clay released another groan. "I want you, April. I want this."

Her knees were looped over his arms, her ass high off the bed, as he pushed that lace aside and ran the tip of his tongue from front to back, pausing to tease her back entrance. He heard her breath catch in her throat and felt the shudder run through her at the unexpected touch of his tongue there.

Grinning, he watched her eyes close as she pushed closer to him. Clay stopped teasing her with his tongue just long enough to ask, "You like that, darlin'?"

She nodded.

"Want more?"

April nodded again, her voice soft, and oh so sexy. "Yes."

Clay used everything he had, teeth, tongue, and hands to torture April, but he avoided the one place he knew she really wanted, no, *needed* to be touched, until both of them couldn't take much more.

He stood again, undid his jeans and noticed the tremble in his hands. Heart pounding, he pushed his pants down over his ankles. Opening the condom box was difficult with shaking hands. Ripping the foil and covering himself wasn't much easier.

Of all the other stuff they'd done before, what he was about to do had only happened in his dreams. Mason may think Clay had slept with April that night he'd gone to her alone, but he hadn't. Yeah, they'd done a lot together, but this, right now, would be their first real time.

April's eyes were barely focused, desire written clearly on her face, as she looked up at him. He pulled off the thong. It had served its purpose of tantalizing him, but now he wanted April, just her, no decorations. Clay wanted to make love to her, pure and simple.

Clay watched her reaction as he pushed against her. She was tight, hot, and sliding into her felt better than he ever imagined. Thrusting into her was even better. Unbelievable, in fact.

He wanted to feel her come around him, and he knew how to make it happen. With one hand he blindly sought for the bottle on the bed, finally opening his eyes to find it in front of Mason. That was when Clay remembered Mason was still in the room, a fact he'd conveniently forgotten in the ecstasy of being buried inside April.

Mason sat in the chair next to the bed, watching Clay and April while stroking his glistening oiled cock. He was getting off from watching them together. That should probably bother Clay, maybe it would later, but somehow right now, it didn't. What it did was make him want to come inside her and claim her for his own.

Clay grabbed the bottle from the end of the bed in front of Mason and quickly drizzled lube onto one hand. He slid one lube-slickened finger easily inside April's ass, almost immediately throwing her over the edge. As Clay pounded them both to completion he heard Mason's now labored breathing culminate in one final grunt as he came, too.

Still throbbing inside April, Clay opened his eyes and watched Mason grab a tissue from the box next to the bed, wipe his hand clean and then strip off his boots, pants and underwear before he crawled onto the bed next to her.

Clay watched Mason kiss the woman who was still breathless from his loving. While still semi-hard and pulsing with aftershocks inside of her, Clay realized the time he'd had to pretend that she was his and his alone had come to an abrupt end. He watched Mason, already hard again, reach for the box of condoms.

Pulling out of April, he took a shaky step back, away

from the bed.

Watching Mason roll on top of April, seeing his hands on her thighs, spreading them so his cock could slide into her where Clay's had just been, had Clay swallowing hard past the lump lodged in his throat. Clay heard April's moan as Mason penetrated her. He watched April raise her hips off the bed as her hands gripped Mason's ass and pulled him into her deeper. He saw her slowly begin to tremble beneath Mason, saw the scratches her nails left on his best friend's skin, and he heard exactly when Mason made her come before his muscles tensed as he thrust into her one last time and then sunk down heavily on top of her.

Clay stood off to the side in the darkness with his stomach feeling as heavy as a rock in his gut and realized they had to get back to the place they'd all been before the word "love" had ever been uttered. That place where he and Mason had both been grateful to simply share her. They would fix it; they had to, because if they continued like this, jealousy would eat him up and destroy them all.

As Clay's mind whirled and his insides churned, April stretched one hand out. "Clay?"

He closed the distance, taking her fingers in his own. "I'm here, darlin'."

"Come to bed."

Mason rolled bonelessly off of April as Clay slipped

onto the rumpled, sweaty sheets on the other side of her.

April yawned and, eyes closed, said sleepily, "I love you both."

Clay gazed down upon the look of total contentment on the face of the woman between them. The irony wasn't lost on Clay. April, who'd had problems with the situation in the beginning, was now perfectly happy loving and being loved by both of them, while Clay and Mason struggled with it all.

He caught Mason's gaze and said, "We love ya too, darlin'."

It was going to be one hell of a summer.

PART II

Chapter Nine

April Dawn, antsy in the chute, snorted out a loud breath when she saw Clay swing up onto the metal rails of the bucking chute. She was his girl. The horse he'd bought green at the stock auction with his saved prize money and trained to be the best damn bucking bronco he'd ever ridden. Yeah, most of the horses that stock trainers preferred to use for rough stock events were geldings, not mares, because they traveled easier in a group. But Clay had loved this horse from the moment he first laid eyes on her—one reason he'd named her after the only other female he'd loved in his life. April Dawn was an angel to handle on the ground, but she was pure hellfire between his legs—another reason she reminded him of his April.

This may be only a practice, but she worked as hard with

the arena empty as she would if the seats were full of thousands of cheering fans.

He spoke softly to her. "Ho, girl. It won't be long now."

Clay swung into his custom-made saddle and slid his boots into the stirrups. He grasped the hack rein in one gloved hand and held the other high in the air. At his nod, the gate opened and April Dawn surged forward, bucking beneath him.

Eight seconds took on all new meaning atop a bronc intent on bucking you off, but when Clay finally heard the buzzer, he was still in the saddle and that was a good thing. He freed his hand from the rope as the pickup man rode up next to him and helped him to the ground. With a grin on his face, Clay landed on his feet (another good thing). He pulled out the mouth guard designed to save his teeth during the ride and stashed it in the pocket of his protective vest as he headed for the exit.

"That is some bronc you trained there, Harris. You interested in selling her yet? I could make her into a star of the PRCA."

Clay raised a brow at the stock contractor next to him. "No, sir. The answer's the same as the last time you asked me."

"I'd pay you well."

"I've got plenty of money," Clay told him.

The man shook his head good-naturedly. "Well, if you change your mind…"

"I know where to find you," Clay finished, then tipped his hat and headed to the stall where April Dawn would have been put away for him by one of the stock handlers.

"Great ride, Clay."

Looking up from beneath the brim of his hat, Clay found one of the pro female barrel racers who'd been dogging his steps for the past few competitions and stifled a groan. "Thanks, Kit."

He kept walking, but unfortunately, she followed. He tried not to notice how low cut her shirt was, but it was hard not to with her throwing her chest out toward his face constantly. "I got some nice cold beer in my trailer, if you wanted to kick back and relax for a bit."

He stared overly hard at his feet as he walked. "Thanks, Kit. I appreciate the offer, but I don't think so."

They'd reached April Dawn's stall. Someone had already unsaddled her for him, probably Mike, one of the other riders he'd gotten friendly with on the circuit. The only thing Clay could do was start grooming her and hope Kit took the hint and went away.

She didn't.

"Who you keeping yourself for, sugar? I never see you with any women and it's not for lack of attention on their part. A good looking, top ranking, pro rider like yourself is a hot commodity, so what has you sleeping alone every night when you could be keeping company with someone?"

Someone meaning her.

Out of the corner of his eye, he could see her checking him out as her eyes moved from his chest, to his chap-covered thighs, to his denim covered ass as he bent over to grab a curry brush. This woman was totally ruining the only serenity Clay could seem to find lately, the time he spent alone with his horse.

He let out a sigh. Maybe she'd leave him be if he told her. "Her name's April."

Kit laughed. "Ah, that is serious."

Clay finally looked at her, brow raised in question.

"A man doesn't name his favorite horse after a woman unless it's true love," she explained.

He had to smile at the truth of her statement, and then the old familiar pain in his heart returned and the smile was gone.

"Hey, Clay. Did you see who you drew for your next ride?"

Clay nodded to his fellow rider on the circuit. "Hey, Mike. Yeah, I saw."

Clay had drawn a beast of a surly bronc by the looks of him. *El Diablo*. "You ever ride him?"

Mike laughed. "Yeah."

Noting the laughter, Clay asked, "You stay on him?"

Mike shook his head. "No." He watched the rider currently getting dumped in the dirt in the arena, then turned to Clay. "El Diablo's on the small side for a saddle bronc. He tends to be a bit more squirrelly than a bigger horse. He likes to twist and turn rather than buck out straight like the big ones do. It makes him harder to control."

"Yeah, but it also gives you a great ride." Clay watched the stock contractors having trouble loading the high-strung El Diablo into the chute.

Mike raised a brow as he followed Clay toward the horse. "Or it gives you a face full of dirt."

Clay grinned. He was up for the challenge.

Kissing the worn photo of April, he shoved it into the back pocket of his jeans. After all these years, it was out of habit and superstition more than anything else that he continued the ritual.

Amid the screams of the spectators in the packed arena, he swung up onto the wall of the bucking chute to look eye to eye with the horse he'd be riding in the competition that night.

The damn thing stared at him now, the whites of his eyes

showing, making him look insane. *El Diablo. The Devil.* That figured. Clay wouldn't be at all surprised to see flames come out of his nose as the horse snorted at him one more time and flung his head.

Clay felt Mike's arm steadying him as he swung onto the devil's back and got situated in the stirrups and saddle. He grabbed the rein tightly and with one hand held up high, nodded.

When the gate opened, El Diablo gave a giant leap in the air, lifting his front legs up and back so violently he threw off his own balance. The last things Clay were aware of was the sensation of the horse falling, his head hitting the dirt and then a feeling of shock as more than half a ton of flailing horseflesh landed on top of him, right before everything finally went black.

Chapter Ten

An explosion rocked the camp right before Mason heard, "Incoming!"

As rounds continued to shake the building, Mason scrambled from his rack where he'd been trying to catch a few hours rest after an all night firefight and grabbed his weapon. He flung open the door, about to run outside into the action when he saw his roommate heading for him. Mason kicked the door wider and held it with one foot so Jenkins could clear the doorway without slowing down.

Adrenaline pumping as hard as it ever had while he was on the back of a bucking bronc, Mason didn't wait for his teammate to gather his weapons, but instead headed for his position. He knew the dusty path to Second Squad's place at the rocks well. They'd sustained enough enemy attacks recently he could run this route in his sleep. In fact, he may have done just that a few times.

First Squad ran for the humvees while Third Squad protected them all with suppressive fire from their position on the rooftops.

Enemy fire peppered the sandbags as Mason reached his position along the rocks. To his right, the squad gunner slammed his machine gun down and immediately began engaging the enemy on the ridgeline. The Afghan National Army was also there, in position right alongside Second Squad. To the left of Mason, one of the ANA soldiers turned and fired a rocket-propelled grenade at another enemy location. Out of his peripheral vision, Mason watched the RPG's trail as it flew in the air toward the enemy.

With a loud blast, the high explosive round the mortar team put into the creek bed with deadly precision to prevent any enemy from sneaking closer, found its mark.

Lobbing grenades at the enemy, Mason heard the whiz of their answering bullets, fired from their cover in the surrounding orchards.

With close air support just minutes away, and First Squad outside the gate assaulting one of the enemy positions, it didn't take long before the attackers gave up the fight, falling back and disappearing again into the mountains. The British fixed wing jets made sure of it by

113

blazing a wide path where the enemy had been just moments before.

Mason leaned back against the rocks, closed his eyes and took a deep breath. Even after years in the Army, and deployments in both Iraq and Afghanistan, he'd never gotten used to the shear physical exhaustion a body felt after the surge of adrenaline wore off.

"Cowboy. You okay?"

Jenkins's voice cut through the fog and Mason opened his eyes, squinting into the glare of the sun.

"Yeah. I'm fine." *Besides hating that damn nickname he'd had since boot camp.* Mason had closed the door on his old life. He was content being a soldier. But it seemed the guys were not going to let him forget his roots so easily.

Mason's roommate hooked a thumb in the direction of the camp. "I'm heading for the room."

"I'll be there in a minute." As soon as he could convince his legs to function again.

Jenkins nodded and was off.

Weary from the longest day in history, Mason finally rose and dragged combat boots that felt at least ten pounds heavier than they had yesterday through the Afghan dust as he headed for his sleeping quarters after a quick trip to the latrine first.

"Mail call, Cowboy," a smiling Jenkins informed him as

Mason opened the door when he finally made it back to his room.

Great.

With a deep sigh, Mason stifled the hope that rose within him. It never failed to rear its ugly head, the hope. Whenever he saw envelopes lying on his bed his hands trembled with the vain expectation one would be from April. Why it still happened, he had no clue, because contact from April had dwindled over the years to nothing but a card at Christmas and on his birthday. Both signed, "Love, April."

Mason gave the small stack a shove with one finger and immediately recognized his mother's handwriting on two of the envelopes, and one colored postcard, which had to be from Clay. He still got mail from Clay, sent from wherever in the country he was competing.

With a sigh, he gathered up the three pieces and flung them on the floor, as if it was the letters' fault they weren't from April.

Jenkins raised a brow and watched them fall without comment. He knew better than to ask. Mason knew Jenkins would be there if he needed him, but roommates didn't butt into each other's personal business unless asked, and thank god for that, because how the hell could Mason ever explain what had happened between the three of them that last summer?

Sure, tales of a drunken threesome would earn him congratulatory high-fives from the rest of the squad, but that wasn't how it had been. Loving a woman and sharing her in every possible way with your best friend nearly every night for months, that tale was more likely to get him ostracized than admired.

The only people he could ever talk to about that summer would be April, who obviously didn't want to hear from him, and Clay, who was too busy traveling and getting famous on the rodeo circuit.

Laying down on his rack with one arm thrown over his face to block out the daylight, Mason succumbed to a restless sleep.

He figured he got about an hour's rest before the dream shook him awake, so vivid he could still see her, feel her, smell her, even with his eyes now wide open. Some soldiers dreamt of the war, but Mason's sleep was haunted instead by visions of the very person who'd forgotten him, but he couldn't forget. In between mail calls, Mason lived to fight, loving the close camaraderie among his squad, but on the days letters arrived and none were from her, the old longing came back, along with the old dreams.

With unbearable twin aches in his heart and his groin, Mason rubbed both hands hard over his face. He heard Jenkins' steady breathing and rose quietly so as not to wake him.

Stepping guiltily over the unread letters from his mother, he did a quick calculation of the time difference between there and home. If one of the phones was both available and working, he would call his mother. He hadn't called home in awhile, anyhow. They'd been too pinned down by enemy contact. Of course, he'd simply tell her he'd been busy and she'd be fine with that, happy just to hear his voice, never able to understand that he liked the thrill of battle, not only for the rush, but also because it blocked out all thoughts of April.

He knew his calling card number by heart and dialed it in quickly, followed by his parents' number. After a few rings, his mother's voice was on the line.

"Hey, Mama. It's me."

"Mason, honey. Thank god you called."

The panic in her voice was unmistakable. "What's wrong? Is Daddy alright?"

Whatever she had to say was not good. He could actually hear her swallow over the phone line as she hesitated before answering. "It's Clay. Honey, Clay's been hurt real bad. He's in a coma in a hospital in Pennsylvania."

Arranging for emergency leave took a little bit of

jumping through hoops and a whole lot of lying. Mason had to convince the people in charge that Clay was not his best friend, but instead his stepbrother from his mother's second marriage. He didn't think God would mind that little fib. It was for a good cause.

The fact Mason rarely, if ever, took leave worked in his favor, as did the fact that his unit was scheduled to be replaced at the forward operating base soon. Mason would have been returning to the garrison in Germany in less than a month anyway. They finally agreed he could get an immediate flight out.

The entire time he was arranging the trip and then finally in the air to the States, Mason felt like the he was racing against the clock. If anything happened before he reached Clay... Mason couldn't even let his mind go there.

He stepped off the flight at the Philadelphia airport and quickly grabbed a plain button-down cotton dress shirt in one of the airport shops. His wardrobe was limited to his uniform and a few old t-shirts nowadays, neither of which was appropriate for the visit to the hospital.

Mason changed in the public restroom. Dressed in his one pair of jeans, cowboy boots he kept more for sentiment than use and his new crisp white shirt, he hailed a cab, a sick feeling in the pit of his stomach as he did so. Now that he was there, he'd have to face seeing Clay in that hospital bed, unconscious, unmoving, looking nothing like the man so full of life he'd left in Oklahoma years ago.

Clay's parents met Mason in the waiting room of the hospital after the nurse went to get them. With a tearful greeting from Mrs. Harris, they ushered him directly into Clay's room. That was not a good sign. It wasn't during the specified visiting hours he'd seen posted and Mason was not family, but the nurses never blinked an eye at their breaking the rules.

The machines, tubes and wires, combined with Clay's pale, bruised face nearly brought Mason to his knees. Even after all he'd seen and done during his time in the infantry, seeing his once vibrant best friend like this knocked the wind right out of him.

Clay's mother, who'd had some time to get used to her son looking so helpless in the hospital bed, wrapped an arm around Mason's back to comfort him. "It's really not as bad as it looks. The doctors explained it to us. It's a medically induced coma. They are keeping him sedated and unconscious on purpose so his body can heal. The doctors are going to bring him out of it today, but then the question is…"

Her voice broke and Clay's father continued for her. "They're not sure if there is damage to his spine. There was a lot of swelling."

Mason swallowed hard. If Clay couldn't ride, he wouldn't want to live. Mason was sure Clay's parents knew that as well as he did.

"There's something I wanted to ask you." Clay's mother pulled herself together and went to the bedside table. She picked up a photo and handed it to Mason.

As if he didn't have enough to deal with already, Mason now was faced with April's smiling image in the torn and tattered picture Mrs. Harris had handed him.

"That was in the pocket of his jeans when they…uh, cut them off of him in the emergency room." Her voice trembled and broke again as her eyes teared up. "I knew they were friends in high school, you all were, but was there more to it, do you know? If he's carried April Carson's photo on him all this time… Should we call to tell her?"

"April doesn't know yet?" He tore his eyes from the photo to look up at the older woman.

Clay's mother shook her head. "Her parents know, of course. The whole town does. Clay was…*is* a bit of a celebrity back home. But April's living in New York now. I can't be sure the Carsons have told her. Should I call and ask them to?"

"Yes, ma'am. April should know." Her name caught in his throat and Mason tried to ignore the pounding of his heart.

She'd come for this. Whether she was with another man now in New York or not, whether she wanted to see Mason or not, she'd come for this. She'd come to see Clay, and Mason would see her again.

Although, now a new suspicion began to arise in his mind as all the facts started to add up. Clay never once mentioned April to Mason in any of his correspondence. Clay carried April's photo in his pocket during competition. Mason rarely heard from April anymore, and when he did, she never spoke of Clay.

Maybe April hadn't found someone new in New York. Maybe April and Clay were a couple and neither of them could face telling him. Clay was making enough money now that he could fly to New York to see her between competitions or fly her to be with him on the road.

But then wouldn't Clay's parents know they were dating? Maybe they kept it secret from their parents so Mason wouldn't accidentally find out.

As jealousy he thought he'd long ago buried reared its head, Mason glanced over to find Clay's father watching him with interest. Mason was not about to elaborate on either his or Clay's relationship with April, past or present, and thankfully, Mr. Harris didn't ask.

Mason turned again to Clay, deathly still in the bed, and his heart felt as if it was being squeezed in a fist. "Mrs.

Harris. You should probably call April's parents as soon as possible."

There was probably not another sound in the world that was both as unnerving and as comforting as the constant *beep, beep, beep* of a hospital monitor. Every blip told Mason that Clay's heart was still beating strong and his body had not given up. But every sound also reminded him that his best friend was still unconscious even though the doctors had weaned him off the drugs keeping him in the medically induced coma. Because neurological tests don't work on a heavily sedated patient, as Clay had been, they had no idea if there was damage.

In the dimly lit room, Mason pulled two chairs close to Clay's bed, slumping low in one while his booted feet occupied the other. It wasn't exactly comfortable, but he'd slept in worse places. He'd convinced Clay's parents to go to their hotel and get some rest, promising he wouldn't leave their son's side. It was an easy vow to make. He'd been away from his friend for too long as it was.

"Well, buddy. It's just you and me, now." Mason leaned his head back against the vinyl chair. He didn't think twice about speaking out loud. Clay had a private room, so he wasn't bothering anyone and it was supposed to be good to talk to patients who were unconscious. More than that, talking aloud somehow comforted Mason.

"I wish you could talk, though. There are a hell of a lot of questions I'd like to ask you, but they'll wait, I suppose." Mason sighed and felt his mind drifting peacefully as he spoke. As usual, when his mind wandered, it traveled immediately to April.

Cracking one eye, he spotted the picture of her on the bedside table. He reached out and picked it up, running a thumb up over the scratched surface.

"So, you and April, huh? It doesn't surprise me. I'd always thought you'd end up together." He let out a long deep breath, eyes still focused on the face in the photo.

"I still think of her, you know. All the time." Mason laughed bitterly. "Dream about her, too. You'd think the dreams would be about just me and her, since they're my dreams and all. But no, you're always there too, Clay old buddy. Just like it was that last night before I left for boot camp."

"Well, that was a really good night."

Mason's boots slipped off the edge of the second chair and crashed to the floor as his eyes flew to the now awake man in the bed next to him. "Clay? Holy crap! You're awake."

Not knowing whether to laugh or cry, Mason was pretty

sure he did both. He grabbed Clay's hand and squeezed it, comforted when it squeezed his back. "I'll get the nurse."

Mason left Clay, who looked totally dazed and still out of it, and ran into the hall, calling for a nurse probably louder than he should given where he was and the late hour.

Even unconscious Clay had charmed the nursing staff, and the night nurse was there in seconds, teary eyed as she checked his vital signs.

When she left to go call Clay's doctor, Mason said, "We need to call your parents."

He reached for the phone when Clay gripped his arm. "Mason, wait. Not yet."

Frowning, Mason nodded. "Okay. But why not?"

"Can I have some water?" Clay's voice sounded scratchy, but that wasn't a surprise considering.

"Sure." Mason held his own bottle of water up to Clay's lips, thinking he'd ask the nurse for a pitcher of ice water when she came back. He noticed Clay's hand come up to try and hold it, only to fall right back down to the bed.

After he'd drank, Mason asked again, "Why don't you want to call your parents? Your mama is so worried…"

"I want to know how bad I am before they get here."

Mason didn't know what to say to that. If Clay didn't know how bad he was, he sure as hell couldn't tell him. Maybe his doctor could answer that question. "Well, how do you feel?"

"Weak as a kitten," Clay answered. "How long have I been out?"

"A couple of days. The docs knocked you out on purpose until the swelling went down. The drugs they used to keep you under have to work their way out of your system. Probably why you still feel weak."

"Damn horse fell on me." Clay shook his head, then his eyes opened wide. "My horse. Is the rodeo still in town? Is someone taking care of April Dawn?"

"April Dawn?"

"I wrote you about her. The mare I bought and trained. She's with me at the arena. She's got a stall in with the barrel horses."

He'd named his horse after April. Mason put the water bottle down and laid his hand over Clay's again, fighting the pain in his heart. "I'll call and find out where she is. I'll check on her personally as soon as I can. I promise."

Seeming satisfied with that, Clay nodded, then flipped the edge of the sheet back.

Mason frowned. "What are you doing?"

"I'm getting out of this bed and seeing if I can walk." Clay used his arms to move to the edge and then realized he was too wired up to move any further. He began pulling off electrodes and was just reaching for the intravenous tube to yank that out of his vein when Mason grabbed his hand.

"Clay! Dammit. Let me get the nurse to do that. God only knows what kind of damage you can do to yourself."

Clay glanced down and peered beneath his hospital gown, then winced. "Alright. Call the nurse, because there's one tube in me I don't think I want to be pulling out myself." He grimaced. "Not that I particularly want some nurse doing it either. But swear to me, Mason. No one calls my parents until I see if I can walk."

"Clay, there was a lot of swelling. It may take some time..."

"Mason, either you're gonna help me on this or get out of my way." He recognized the determination in Clay's face.

Mason nodded. "I'm with you, but we do this the right way or you'll damage yourself. Let me get the nurse. We'll get those tubes out of you, call your parents and then we'll see what you can do *after* the doc see you. Okay?"

Clay nodded and leaned back against the pillow, looking like he wanted to fight but knew he'd lose. "Okay."

Using his usual charm, Clay easily convinced the nurse that he'd be a good boy and eat and drink anything she brought him, and even pee in the bedpan if she would take out the IV and catheter. Clay probably could have charmed her into just about anything while never mentioning that the moment she left the room, he was going to try and walk.

Rough Stock

Over Mason's dead body! That wasn't going to happen until the doc evaluated Clay's injuries. Then, whatever the damage was, they'd deal with it.

Chapter Eleven

"Walk for me."

April did as she was told and walked across the apartment. Since it took her only a few steps to traverse the incredibly small room, she spun and made the return trip while Ben sat on the futon sofa/bed.

"Gorgeous. Absolutely gorgeous." Ben clapped his hands together. "Now, take it off so I can shorten the halter top strap an inch."

April laughed and glanced down at the neckline that plunged deep between her breasts and exposed her nearly to the stomach. "You really think an inch is going to make a difference?"

She unfastened the neck of the dress and let the blood red satin pool to the floor at her feet, before stepping out of it in nothing but underwear and heels.

Ben grabbed the dress and shook it out. "An inch will make the difference between those luscious tits of yours staying in the dress or falling out of it at the party tonight." He raised a brow at her expectantly.

"An inch it is then!"

April put her push-up bra back on and pulled a silk tank over her head while Ben's gaze swept the apartment, the entirety of which was comprised of a single room the size of her bedroom in her parents' house, a microwave and a tiny bathroom that she strongly suspected had once been a closet, since the apartment didn't have one of those.

"Why do you insist on living in this...*place*?"

She had a feeling Ben had another word he would have rather used. "Because it's all I can afford at the moment."

New York rentals cost a fortune. As it was, April didn't have cable television, or a phone or internet in her apartment. In fact, she only managed to have a cell phone because her boss Christian paid for that. And damn, she'd have to remember to plug it in and charge it because it had been dead for awhile now, but since she'd been with Christian at the theater for about twenty hours a day for the past week as opening night approached, she didn't exactly need the phone. He could just yell if he needed her.

Ben suspiciously eyed the linen pants she'd just pulled

on to go with the silk tank and designer shoes. "You had enough money to put that outfit together, I see."

April scowled and pointed to each of the three pieces of her wardrobe in turn, starting at her feet and working her way up. "Shoes, sample sale; pants, used from a thrift shop; and top, clearance rack."

Ben smiled at her lovingly. "My little bargain shopper! And I guess it doesn't hurt to have a perfect, sample-sized body, either."

She let out a laugh. "Yeah, yeah. Make fun of me, but if it wasn't that my best friend was a clothing designer, I'd have nothing decent to wear for the party tonight."

He took a step closer and kissed her, softly, gently, on the lips. "And if my best friend wasn't the personal assistant to the hottest new director on Broadway, I wouldn't be invited to the party tonight, so we're even."

April sighed and thought of all the many times she'd raided the sample rack at Ben's studio when she had a last minute fashion emergency. "I guess so." But sometimes it didn't feel so even.

Taking a step back, Ben glanced at his watch. "I'll run home and knock out the alteration quick. I'll bring the dress tonight and you can change for the party at the theater, I guess?"

She nodded. "I left a ticket for tonight's show under

your name at the window."

"Thanks, sweetie." Ben waited for her to unlock the chain and two deadbolts before he planted another quick kiss on her. "See you later."

April nodded. "Later." Then closed the door and glanced down at her own watch—and noticed exactly how late it was. She needed to get to the theater. Christian would probably be flipping out today from the pressure of opening night.

April scrambled to gather a clutch purse, pantyhose, makeup, and jewelry to go with the dress for the party later and flung it all into her tote bag. She was halfway out the door when she remembered her phone. No time to charge it now. She'd have to plug it in at the theater. Grabbing both the cell and the charger, she added them to the contents of her bag and was out the door in a New York minute.

Opening night passed in a blur, between Christian's near meltdown when he heard the lead actor had a sore throat, to the computer glitch that had oversold the house by ten percent more seats than actually existed. But amazingly, somehow it all worked out. Dressed in Ben's creation that had everyone in the room drooling—the straight men because of the cleavage and the gay men and women because the design was simply scrumptious—all that was left for April to do was enjoy the party and wait for the reviews to come out in the next day's edition.

Oh, and she should probably eventually listen to the five voicemails she'd noticed on her cell phone when she finally charged it and turned it on back at the theater. She pulled the cell out of her bag and punched in her code. Holding it to her ear, April smiled and nodded as Ben held up his empty glass and pointed toward the bar. She could definitely use another drink after the week she'd had.

When her father's voice sounded on the message, April expected it to just be the usual, "How are you?" phone call, but what he said had her feeling weak in the knees. Trembling, she grabbed onto the lapel of Ben's tuxedo when he returned to her carrying two martinis.

He frowned, put the drinks down on a nearby bus tray and held her by both arms while she listened to one message after another. By the last two voicemails, her father was simply asking if she was getting his messages and begging her to call. What else was there left for him to say? The big bomb had been dropped during the first three times he'd called.

The first one had been relatively casual. "We just got word that Clay Harris took a fall and was injured in the competition in Philadelphia. We're not sure how bad it is."

The second was far more ominous. "We just heard that Clay's in a coma. We'll let you know more as soon as we can."

But it was the next one that tore her apart. "Mrs. Harris just called from the hospital in Philly. Um, April, we all know you're busy, but she thinks you need to get over there if you can, as soon as possible. Here's the information…"

She lowered the phone after the final voicemail and sunk against Ben's chest as the intensity of the feelings she'd managed to tamp down for all these years bombarded her at once.

"April, sweetie, are you okay?"

She shook her head. "Get me out of here. Please, Ben. Now."

"Sure."

He parted the crowd and soon had her out the door and seated in his car, while she did nothing but stumble after him in a daze, her phone still clutched in one hand and her purse in the other. Ben reached over from the driver's seat and took both from her, stashing them in the console before taking her now ice-cold hands in his warm ones.

"Tell me."

And she did. Sobbing so hard at times she couldn't form words, April told him the entire story of that summer. Every detail, things she'd never told another living soul. Things she'd managed lately to pretend didn't happen as she somehow forced closed the door on that chapter of her life.

She'd had to block it all out, it was the only way she could move forward. She finished, exhausted, broken, and in more pain than she thought possible.

Ben listened silently until she was done, then he gave her hands a squeeze, turned in his seat and started the car. He pulled away from the curb and she assumed he was bringing her back to her apartment, until he turned onto the highway, heading for the bridge.

"Where are we going?"

"Philadelphia."

"What?"

"April, there's a man you still obviously love lying in a hospital bed and he needs you. Once we get out of the city, there should be no traffic this time of night. We can be there in under two hours if I speed."

Her tears started anew. "You'd do that for me. Drive me all the way to Philadelphia?"

"Of course I would. I love you."

April swallowed hard. "And the rest. You haven't said anything about that." She bit her lip and waited as he merged into the fast lane before finally answering her.

"Sweetie, I'm a gay man who lives in New York City and works in the fashion industry. Did you really think that a woman loving and being loved by two men in a caring, committed relationship would be scandalous to me?"

134

When he put it that way, it didn't sound that bad. If only she'd had the guts to confess it all to him when they'd first met freshman year in college. She could have used his wisdom and comfort then. It would have saved her, all of them, a lot of heartbreak. But she had to remember, New York was not Oklahoma and she doubted anyone back home would be as understanding as Ben if they knew the truth.

"Thank you, Ben."

He waved off her gratitude with one hand. "I'm not saying I'm not jealous as hell that you had not one, but two hot rodeo cowboys dedicated to pleasing you both in bed and out, but I guess I'll get over it. Although, when you choose a man who thinks eight seconds is a long time, perhaps you need two of them. Hmm?"

Ben grinned at her and April felt her cheeks flush hot at the mention of the three of them in bed. He must have sensed her discomfort because he laid one hand on her knee. "Don't get embarrassed, sweetie. I've got far more sordid secrets in my past, believe me. Including a ménage-a-trois. Two women and me."

Glancing at him with a raised brow, April asked, "Two *women*?"

Ben laughed. "Yeah, I went through a period when I was trying to be straight. One woman didn't do it for me so I thought I would try two. Had to get myself drunk as shit to

135

do it, too. As you can see, it didn't work."

She saw the good-natured grin Ben shot her before directing his eyes back to the dark highway. "So, do you think your two cowboys have any gay rodeo friends they can fix me up with?"

And for the first time since getting the phone message that was bound to change her life whether she wanted it to or not, April laughed.

Chapter Twelve

"You sure you are ready for this, Clay?"

"Yes." Clay flipped the sheet and blanket back.

Clay may be ready, but Mason wasn't. "But you only woke up like twenty-four hours ago. Don't you want to rest some more?"

"I slept all damn day! The doc said things looked good. My parents finally went back to the hotel for the night. We're doing this now, Mason."

Mason sighed. He knew Clay when he was determined. He would do this with or without Mason's help. Not knowing whether he was being a good friend or an idiot who was helping Clay do more damage to himself, Mason let Clay wrap one arm around his neck while he supported Clay's weight with an arm on his waist. The fact Clay had the power to swing his legs over the edge of the bed was encouraging. If he were paralyzed, or if there was spinal cord damage, that would have been impossible. Right? Although, what the hell did Mason know, he was no doctor.

"Clay, are you sure you want to try this?"

"Mason. Shut up and start walking." A bead of sweat glistened on Clay's brow.

"You're in pain. I can tell."

"*You're* gonna be in pain if you don't get me across this room."

With a sigh, Mason took one step forward and watched as Clay's foot moved to follow. Clay's weight shifted to the front foot and Mason decided that constituted one full step.

"See, that's great! You took a step. Now let's get you back to bed."

Clay ignored him and took another step, then another, before he reached out and grabbed the end of the bed frame, rattling the metal as he leaned on it heavily. Mason stood behind him, braced and ready to catch Clay if he fell. But he didn't. His face was bright red, his jaw set firm, but Clay stood under his own power.

Letting out a shaky laugh, Clay turned his head to look at Mason. "All right. It's not so bad. You can get me back to bed now."

Breathing a huge sigh of relief, Mason resisted the urge

to hoist Clay up and bodily put him back in bed, and instead moved under his arm again, letting Clay lean on him as he worked his way back onto the mattress.

Clay looked up and over Mason's shoulder and his breath suddenly caught in his throat.

Concerned, Mason leaned in. "What's wrong? Shit, I knew this was a bad idea."

When no answer followed, he followed Clay's gaze and there in the doorway was none other than April. A day late, but there, nonetheless.

Seeing her standing in front of him after all these years took his breath away. She looked the same while at the same time, totally different. Her skin was paler and more porcelain and her hair darker than he'd ever seen it, as if she hadn't been out in the sun in a long time. Her face had been pretty before, but now she had a mature sophisticated beauty that came either from getting older, or the killer red dress that revealed far too much of her body for Mason's liking.

Tears in her eyes, she took one step forward into the room, and then hesitated. When neither of them said a word, she spoke. "The nurse said I could come in. She said she recognized me but I didn't know what she meant."

She twisted her fingers together nervously. A few years ago Mason would have gone to her and held her until that frightened, uncertain look left her face. Now, he didn't move, except to glance at Clay, who also had been strangely quiet. Mason wondered about that.

Looking more uncomfortable with each passing moment, April kept talking. "My father said you were in a coma."

Finally, Clay spoke. "I woke up."

Mason raised a brow. Perhaps he'd been wrong about April and Clay, because this was not the way a man should act when first seeing his girlfriend after he'd stared death in the face and won.

April's gaze shifted to Mason and he felt as uncomfortable as she looked. "Mason."

He gave her the smallest of nods. "April." Of all of the times he'd dreamed of seeing her again, now that she was here, he had nothing to say.

"I'm surprised to see you here." Her voice sounded so small.

"I bet you are." Mason's response came out sharper than he'd meant it to and her saw her react to it. Her eyes filled, glistening with unshed tears.

He watched her swallow. "I'm glad you're okay, Clay." Then she turned and ran out of the room.

Mason let out a long, slow curse under his breath, then looked up to find Clay shaking his head.

"All the times I hoped and prayed she'd come walking

into a room, and now that she did…"

Mason nodded to his friend. "I know."

"She doesn't return any of my phone calls, she hasn't written since a card last Christmas."

"I know, Clay. Not to me, either."

"Why?" Clay asked.

Mason laughed. "Hell if I know. I thought it was because she was dating you and didn't want to tell me."

Clay frowned. "I would have told you. I don't take the coward's way out, Mason. Never have, never will."

"I know that, and I apologize. Hard to be rational about things like this though."

"Yeah, I know." Clay shook his head again. "Go after her, Mason."

"What? Why?"

"Because I have a feeling we're gonna be really sorry later if we don't, and I'm not exactly up for a sprint so it has to be you."

"Are you sure?"

Clay nodded.

Mason let out a breath. "Okay. I'll be back."

He ran out into the hall and turned for the exit, figuring he'd catch her at the elevator, but when he passed the glass windows of the waiting room, he skidded to a stop. April was inside, weeping in the arms of a man who looked like he'd stepped off the pages of some magazine with his perfect hair and black tuxedo, complete with bow tie.

Mason stood transfixed, staring at what he assumed was the main reason for April's absence in their lives, when she looked up and saw him. He was still deciding on whether to turn around and go back to Clay's room, or stand his ground when April sped past him and disappeared into the ladies' room and her boy toy approached him. Then, it was too late, because Mason never backed down from a fight.

The man was taller than Mason, and since he stood six foot one without his boots on, that was saying something. Perhaps there were heels on those black tuxedo shoes.

"You must be Mason."

"I must be. And who might you be?" *As if I don't know.*

"Ben. Ben Michaels."

Mason noted how *Ben, Ben Michaels* didn't extend his hand to shake, which was fine with him. He had no intention of shaking the hand he could vividly picture roaming all over April's body. He didn't even have to imagine it, since that dress she was wearing was backless as well as practically frontless, and Ben Ben's hands had been all over her, "comforting" her, Mason supposed.

Once upon a time, that had been his job. His and Clay's. Obviously she'd found one guy who could do the job it had taken them both to accomplish back when they were eighteen. Mason scowled at the thought.

"You know something, Mason? That girl dropped everything in New York and came here to see your friend because he needed her. And when she gets here, you make her cry and then have the nerve to stand there with that puss on your face. You don't deserve her."

Mason stood tall, right up in Ben Ben's face. "What the hell do you know about anything?"

His face showed a look of satisfaction. "I know everything."

Mason snorted out a laugh. "I seriously doubt that."

Ben Ben laughed himself. "Well, it was a long drive but I can probably remember most of the important details. Let's see, you two had sex the first time in a lake by moonlight. Very romantic, I might add. And then you, she and Clay all…"

Mason held up one hand to stop him.

Ben paused, one brow raised. "What? You don't want to hear what she told me about Clay?"

No, he really did not, but Mason couldn't form words at the moment.

She had told this guy everything. April, who had trouble opening up to Mason and Clay that summer, had spilled all of her secrets and theirs to this man who obviously meant more to her than they had.

Mason swallowed hard and figured he had nothing left to lose. Since he'd already lost April, he may as well go for it. "So if you know so much, tell me this. Why did she stop writing to both of us? Why didn't she call? Why did she act as if nothing had ever happened? Huh? I'm betting it was because of you."

Ben's face softened. "I don't know why she didn't keep in touch, but I can assure you, it had nothing to do with me."

Ah, so Ben Ben was a new addition in April's life. It must have been another guy, then.

Mason sighed, feeling guilty for blaming the messenger. "Look, I didn't mean to make her cry, it's just…"

"You're still in love with her and it hurts?"

God, Mason hated opening his soul to anyone, but he definitely was not going to do it for this guy. "Whatever. Look, you'll take care of her and make sure she gets home okay tonight, right?"

Ben laughed sadly. "I can make sure she gets home, but I'm not the one who can make her okay. You and Clay have to do that."

Mason frowned. "Haven't you been listening? She doesn't want us. She hasn't for a long while. I don't know what she wants."

"Then find out."

Shaking his head, Mason stared at this man before him.

"You're telling me to make a play to take your girlfriend away from you?"

At that, Ben let out a deep laugh, straight from the belly. "April is not my girlfriend. She's my friend."

With one brow cocked, Mason pulled up one lip in a sneer. "Yeah, like she was just Clay's and my friend, too."

Ben Ben shook his head emphatically. "Not the same thing at all."

Mason continued to stare at the lunatic before him until Ben finally said, "You really haven't figured it out yet, have you? I guess it's true what they say about the turnip truck."

"Excuse me?"

"Nothing, just me being a snide New Yorker. Look, Mason, sweetie. I'm gay. The only way April could be my girlfriend would be if she strapped a dick onto that hot little body of hers. And the only reason I know she has a hot body is because she wears the clothes I design for her so divinely. Now, if *you'd* be willing to join us in bed, I'm sure I could rise to the occasion and perform adequately for her…"

Mason skipped right over the fact Ben Ben was baiting him with his bawdy come on, he jumped straight past the relief that he wasn't April's boyfriend because that didn't mean she didn't have one stashed back in New York, and instead he focused on the one thing that was most important. "You designed that…*dress* she's wearing?"

Ben nodded.

Mason scowled. "Well, next time, try putting a front and a back in it, okay?"

Laughing until he had to wipe his eyes, Ben finally found enough breath to say, "You cowboys are absolutely precious!"

With no clue how to respond to that, Mason turned. "You should go check on April."

Ben grabbed his arm. "I'll go in a sec. Listen, Mason, seriously. I can tell you this. I've known her since college. Whatever kept April away from you two, it wasn't loving another man. I promise you that."

Mason shrugged callously, letting his eyes roam over Ben Ben's impeccable and very expensive-looking tux. "Then the answer is clear. We country boys were good enough for her then, but we aren't anymore. That's fine. Tell her I wish her well."

He turned and walked back to Clay's room.

Chapter Thirteen

Surrounded by the antiseptic smell of the hospital, April stared at the puffy-eyed, tear-streaked face reflected back at her in the mirror.

The door swung open, and although she expected it to be one of the female nurses, instead Ben stood in the doorway. "May I come in?"

"I'm alone in here, if that's what you're asking."

He shook his head and stepped inside, letting the door shut completely behind him. "Well, that, and I guess I'm asking if you want company."

April released a short laugh. "Sure. Why not."

Behind her, Ben's hands began stroking her bare arms as he met her gaze in the mirror. "Wanna talk about it?"

"What's there to talk about? They both hate me."

Ben shook his head. "No. I don't think so. I talked to the angry one. Mason."

April laughed bitterly at the apt description Ben had used. "And?"

"He's hurt, he's angry, but it doesn't stem from hate, April. It's love. Straight men don't know how to deal with emotions like that." He turned her to face him, and she leaned back against the sink so she could look up at his face. "He said you stopped writing or calling them both."

"It's complicated, Ben. You wouldn't understand."

"Try me."

She sighed. The middle of the night in a hospital public restroom was not the time and place she pictured confessing her sins, but then again, there would be no good time for this. "That first time with Mason…"

Ben nodded.

"We didn't use anything."

April watched understanding dawn on her best friend's face as he took a deep breath in and let it out slowly. "Oh. How did you handle it?"

"I didn't. I ignored that I only spotted but never really got my period that summer. I told myself it was just nerves or something. I figure I was only two months along when I left for school and I wasn't really showing so the guys never suspected. Then, when I got to New York for school…"

She swallowed hard. "One night I had a fever and chills, cramping and stomach pains and I had to keep running to the toilet… I thought at first it was a stomach flu. Then the pain was bad enough I thought it was appendicitis. My roommate brought me to the infirmary on campus and they told me I'd miscarried. A part of me was grateful I'd lost it, but a part of me was grieving over a baby I didn't even know existed. Then they said it was still inside me and they had to do a D and C. The whole thing was horrible, Ben."

He wrapped his arms around her and held her close. "Oh, sweetie. I'm sorry you had to go through that all alone. You were so young."

"It felt like God was punishing me for doing what I did, what we all had done together."

"That's bull, April. No god would blame a woman for loving as deeply as I know you loved those two."

April leaned her forehead against his chest and rolled it from side to side in disagreement. "I'm not so sure about that, Ben."

"So that was why you severed contact with them?"

She raised her head again. "I didn't *sever contact*, I brought things back to where they should have been before I messed them up, just friends."

"Only they didn't know what you were doing or why. You need to tell them. This is tearing you apart, and them too, from what I've seen of the pissed off cowboy out there."

Telling the story to Ben, who was sweet and understanding and loved her unconditionally, had been draining enough. She couldn't imagine having to repeat the tale, and to the two angry men she'd faced in that hospital room. "What would be the point? So much time has passed. They have both hated me for so long. Even if I do tell them now, then what?"

"Then, you see what happens. I'm not saying they'll come to you with open arms, but at least maybe the hurt can start to heal for all three of you."

The door swung open again and this time, it was a nurse. "Oh, hi there! Aw, don't look so upset. The doctor was just in with him a few hours ago and he says he's doing just fine. And I'm sure you being here will speed his recovery right along."

April frowned. Why did the nurse think that? And why had she acted like she knew her before? "Um, when I arrived, you said you recognized me. Why was that?"

The nurse stepped to the sink and rinsed out her coffee mug, catching April's eye in the mirror. "The photo, of course. When they brought Mr. Harris in, your picture was in his back pocket. When his parents arrived we gave it to them with the rest of his things and they said you two had been together since high school."

Grabbing a paper towel from the wall dispenser, the chatty nurse dried her mug and hands.

"I married my high school sweetheart, so I understand, believe me. You must have been going crazy that you couldn't get here right away. Anyway, you're here now. I need to get back to my station." She smiled prettily and was gone.

When they were alone again, April looked up to see Ben's raised brow. "Carrying around your picture in his pants doesn't sound like the actions of a man 'in hate' to me."

When she didn't move, Ben shook his head. "Stubborn right to the end. I'm beginning to think that's an Oklahoma trait. Come on, sweetie. Splash water on your face and go see that man of yours."

April scowled. "He's not mine." *Anymore*.

Ben shook his head at her. "We'll see."

For some unexplainable reason, April did as she was told. She washed the tears from her face and then allowed Ben to steer her out of the bathroom. He gave her a small push in the direction of Clay's room and motioned toward the waiting room. "I'll be in there enjoying last year's *People Magazine*."

April's heart warmed. "Thank you, Ben."

He grinned. "No problem."

Knowing her friend was behind her was probably the only thing that kept her walking towards her two former friends. Her whole body shook as she reached the doorway. She could see Clay in the bed sipping at a cup with a straw. Mason was there too, sitting in the chair with his arms braced on his knees in such a familiar pose April felt transported back through the years.

Mason saw her first and straightened up in the chair. Clay noticed her and pushed his cup further back on the bed tray. "Told you she wouldn't just leave," he said to Mason in a low, satisfied voice.

Like Mason's mannerisms, Clay's attitude hadn't changed at all since high school either. Clay's comment was answered with a scowl from Mason.

April still hovered in the doorway, suddenly feeling self-conscious as she noticed Clay's eyes consuming her exposed cleavage. She crossed her arms in front of her. "Um, can I come in?"

"Sure, darlin'. Mason, give her a chair."

Mason's brows shot up but he stood as Clay asked, shoved a chair in her direction, then he moved toward the door. "I'm gonna go to the arena and check on your horse. I'll be back later."

The unspoken words *when she's gone* broke April's heart. She moved far to the side so he wouldn't have to squeeze past her to get out of the room.

Clay frowned. "Mason, it's the middle of the night!"

He paused in the doorway. "So? The cabs will still be running, and you and I both know that even though the competition is over, the stock contractors will still be around, keeping an eye on the animals. Besides, I thought you were worried about her."

Clay sighed. "I am. All right. Do what you got to do. And while you're there, get someone to show you my trailer and pick me up some clothes. I don't intend on staying in this gown thing. I saw my keys in the drawer, and take my identification so you don't have trouble getting back to the stock pens."

Mason nodded, went to the bedside table drawer, opened it and grabbed an ID card and a set of keys. Then, without so much as goodbye, he was gone, leaving April alone with Clay. She'd intended on talking to them both together, it seemed like the right thing to do, but she realized having to face only Clay would be easier. Of the two, he definitely seemed to be the more receptive.

"Sit down, darlin', and tell me, where were you and your friend coming from when you came here instead? Because that dress sure is pretty enough for a party."

April sat but kept her back straight, wary of the gaps in the dress if she slouched. "It was a party, and he's just a friend, Clay. Nothing more."

Clay smiled at that. "I know. Mason told me. And I have to tell you I'm relieved your date is gay, since I've held the title of your friend and I know what can happen."

She ignored his teasing. "Clay. I'm so sorry."

He shook his head. "No, darlin'. I'm sorry. I wasn't very nice to you before. You kind of took me by surprise. Mason wasn't very nice, either, but he can do his own apologizing."

"Mason is so angry."

Clay nodded. "Yeah. But it's only because he still cares about you."

She doubted that. "Why are you being so nice?"

"The doctor says it's a miracle there's no permanent damage. Someone upstairs saw fit to give me a second chance. I reckon it's only fair I do the same for you." Clay stared at her boldly. "Besides, you're not so easy to fall out of love with."

Clay still loved her. That broke her and the tears started fresh. "Oh, Clay. I have something to tell you."

And that's when Clay's nurse walked in, greeted them both cheerfully, handed him a pill, and gave April a reprieve from her confession for the time being.

Chapter Fourteen

"Well, you're not Clay, sugar, but I'm sure not complaining about the view."

Mason unhooked his boot heel from the gate of April Dawn's stall and turned to find the source of the voice.

She smiled at him and extended her hand. "I'm Kit, a friend of Clay's. And who might you be?"

Mason shook her hand and had to work to disengage his fingers from her grip afterwards. "Mason."

"Ah, the Army friend. Nice to meet ya."

Maybe she was a friend of Clay's, since she knew his name. Glancing quickly at the expanse of exposed breast, Mason had to wonder how good a friend she was.

Kit cocked a head toward the mare, who'd accepted Mason's presence as if she'd known him her whole life. Clay always did have a knack for picking the best horses. "I've been keeping an eye on her for him. And I kept that stock contractor away from her, too. He's got it in his head that now that Clay's hurt, he'll be willing to sell her."

"I'm sure Clay will appreciate that."

"How's he doing? I've been meaning to get to the hospital but...to be perfectly honest, I couldn't bring myself to go."

Mason nodded, understanding totally. If it had been anyone else besides Clay laid up there, he might not have willingly gone himself. "He woke up yesterday, and tonight he walked a bit."

Kit's eyes opened wide. "Oh, thank the Lord! I knew nothing would keep that boy down. That's a relief to hear though. Thank you."

Mason accepted the thanks with a single nod of his head. He reached out and rubbed April Dawn's ear, and she stood and happily let him. "When are you all moving on to the next city?"

"Tomorrow. When's Clay fixing to join us again? I can take care of April for a bit if you need. I'm traveling with a two horse trailer with only my barrel horse in it."

"He won't be back to riding on the circuit for a bit, I think. The doc wants him in physical therapy but, knowing Clay, he won't stand for that. He'll try to push it too fast and do damage to himself. I figure I'll drive his trailer and the mare back home to Oklahoma for him and he'll have to follow whenever the doc says he can fly. That way he won't be tempted to catch up with the rest of you on the circuit."

Kit grinned. "You're a smart one, and a good friend. He's lucky to have you."

Mason rolled his eyes. Some friend he was, purposely not coming home to the States and not seeing Clay for years because of April. "Not really. Um, do you know which trailer is his? I need to get him some things."

"I surely do."

Mason raised a brow at that, again wondering at Kit's familiarity with both Clay and his trailer. She answered his unspoken question. "Don't be getting the wrong idea. I've never been a guest there the way you're thinking. Not for lack of trying, mind you. The flame he's harboring for that April girl is a mighty strong one to keep him out of my bed. You got any old flames, Mason?"

Little did she know. "Unfortunately, yes, ma'am, I do."

Kit looked him up and down shamelessly. "That's too bad. Come on. I'll show you to the trailer."

Mason locked the door of Clay's trailer, pocketed the keys and headed for the well-lit entrance of the hospital.

He'd decided to drive the trailer back to the hospital rather than have to take a taxicab back and forth, which could get expensive on an Army paycheck. On top of that, Clay had a real nice set-up. Mason could sleep there rather than in the hospital chair and still be near Clay, whenever he finally got to sleep tonight.

As he neared the front door and saw April and Ben standing outside, Mason nearly turned right around and headed back to the trailer, but chances were they'd see his retreat, and he had promised Clay he'd be right back.

Close enough to them, Mason could hear Ben and April speaking.

"I've got today's clothes, my phone and charger and makeup. I'll just sleep here in the lounge tonight and take a train back to the city sometime tomorrow. I can't leave until I talk to them both."

Mason slowed down and finally came to a dead stop in the shadows.

"Are you sure? I could get us a hotel room for the night here in Philly. Or I could drive you home and we can come back tomorrow after you've changed and rested."

"No, I won't let you do that. You've been too generous already and I know you have to get back to Burberry."

He waved a hand. "So there's some dog poo on the floor when I get home. I'll live! Honestly."

April laughed and took a large bag from Ben's hand. "Thank you, but no. Go. Okay? I love you."

"I love you, too." Ben bent and kissed her. It was quick and chaste, and, gay or not, Mason was jealous as all hell of him.

Ben headed for the other side of the parking lot and April turned to go back into the hospital when Mason stepped out of the shadows. Surprise showed on her face as she stopped. "You're back."

Hands shoved deep into his jeans pockets, Mason nodded. "I told Clay I'd be back."

"Look, Mason, can we talk?"

"April, I get it. There's no need to explain. Clay and I are rough stock and you're looking for certified and purebred."

She frowned at him. "That's not it at all. If you let me…"

He threw one hand up. "I don't want to hear any explanations. You made your choice. As soon as Clay is up and around again, I'll go back to my unit, you'll go back to whoever in New York and we'll never have to be bothered with each other again."

"When exactly did you become so heartless?" Teary-eyed yet again, April shook her head and reached for the handle of the glass door. As he watched her waiting for the elevator inside the lobby, he whispered, "Right about the time you crushed my heart."

With a sigh, he entered himself, and in an act that could only be called childish if he were willing to put a name to it, he took the stairs rather than wait for the elevator with April.

Mason would tell Clay that his horse was fine, feign exhaustion, and head back to the trailer to sleep. He'd deal with all the rest in the morning.

Chapter Fifteen

Once Mason had come and gone again like a cyclone and he and April were alone once more, Clay turned to her. She looked near to dropping from exhaustion. He patted the edge of the bed.

"Crawl on up here, darlin'. That chair's no place to spend the night."

Looking so tired she'd agree to anything about now, April pulled herself onto the mattress and settled against Clay's shoulder with a sigh. Then she lifted her head. "Am I hurting you?"

He shook his head and pulled her head back down. "No, not a bit. And even if you were, the view makes up for it."

She looked down and adjusted the front of the dress so it once again covered her exposed breast, then frowned at him.

"I guess you are feeling better. And I should change out of this dress and into real clothes. It's not even mine."

"Well, I don't know who it belongs to, but leave it on a bit longer, because I surely do like it."

He felt her smile and his heart lifted. Her skin felt so inviting and it had been so long since he'd touched her, he couldn't stop his hand from running up and down her arm as he itched to explore more. "You were about to tell me something before we were interrupted. Do you feel like talking now?"

She shook her head. "No. Can we talk in the morning?"

"Sure. I'll be here, I reckon." Clay heard her small laugh at his little joke. "So, you feel like kissing instead?"

Against all hope, she hesitated a beat and then replied, "Do you?"

He suddenly found it hard to breath. "I've never stopped wanting to kiss you."

She turned her face toward his and their eyes met for a moment before he leaned down and brushed her lips with his.

One small kiss wasn't enough. It never had been between them. He tangled his hand in her hair and the familiar feel of that act had him groaning as he plunged his tongue into her mouth. She turned and threw one leg over him, straddling his thighs and grabbing his face with both of her hands.

"Am I hurting you?" she asked breathlessly.

"No," he could barely answer before his mouth was on hers again. His hands easily parted the front of the dress and found her bare breasts aroused to sharpened peaks.

Clay broke the kiss and bent his head to roll one hard nipple between his lips. April held his head closer and the sound of pleasure coming out of her sent a shiver straight through him.

He moved back to claim her mouth again—just as the door opened.

"Oh, boy. Excuse me." They both looked up at the embarrassed nurse as she threw her hand over her eyes. "I just came to check if you needed anything, but I see you're fine. I'll just, ah, close the door."

When she'd left, Clay laughed and April, who hadn't grown out of her tendency to blush, crawled off of his lap, red-faced. "I am so embarrassed."

"Don't be. We were only kissing."

Thankfully she stayed on the bed next to him and didn't flee to the chair. Clay wrapped one arm around her shoulder and held her close, his other hand playing with the soft material of the dress covering her legs. "And you know what?"

She shook her head.

"At least now, I know that my dick still works." He waggled his eyebrows at her, more relieved at that fact than his joking let on. "Wanna see?"

"No!" Her face flushed.

Afraid to push her too far too soon, not to mention he wasn't exactly sure he had it in him to make love to a woman right now, Clay joked, "Oh, all right. I should probably save that for when we have some privacy anyway. Don't want to frighten the nurse if she comes in again."

He looked down and enjoyed her blush, then a thought hit him. "You are going to stick around for a little while, right?"

He had both of his best friends back and he wasn't willing to part with either of them just yet.

"I don't know that I can. I have a job in New York. My boss will need me."

He felt his heart fall. "Oh, okay. I understand."

She was quiet for a second before she finally said, "Let me see what I can do."

"I can't ask for more than that, now can I?" Clay smiled.

They stayed like that in silence for a few minutes, just leaning on each other.

"April?"

"Yeah?"

"I can't be this close to you and not touch you."

164

"Do you want me to move back to the chair?"

"Hell, no. I want to touch you. Can I? Nothing more, just touch you."

He felt her take a shaky breath. "Okay."

His hand bunched up the fabric and uncovered her thighs so he could run his hands over the long, lean muscles he remembered the feel of so well. *How many times had these legs been wrapped around him that summer?* He couldn't begin to count.

Clay felt April shudder as his fingers ran up and down her thigh. He leaned in for a kiss and she whispered, "You said touching, not kissing."

"Kissing is touching, just with the lips. Now, hush up."

After a few minutes, she was putty in his hands, just as she always had been. Her legs, which had started out locked tightly together, relaxed and spread for him.

"I've missed you." Clay ran a finger over the dampened crotch of her panties.

She drew in a breath. "You missed the sex."

He shook his head and repeated the touch, loving how her body jerked when he did. "No. Not just the sex, I missed all of you."

"What you are doing isn't exactly proving that."

His finger pushed aside the elastic and slid into her slick warmth, causing his own heart to speed at the familiar feel of her. He slipped it out again and began to circle her clit as he watched her mouth open and her eyes drift close.

"Not true at all, darlin'." He added two fingers inside of her and slowly began to work her G spot as he spoke. "I do miss all of you, but this part, the sex, *this* we're good at. Even when everything else was shit, the times when you were mad at us or I was jealous of Mason, or you refused to talk about things, this between us was always good, and it made everything else seem better."

Her hips were off the bed, pushing against his hand. "So sex is like a medicine that cures all ills?" Her voice was breathless as she spoke.

"Mmm, hmm. Exactly." She started to shake but hadn't quite gone over the edge, and he really wanted her to, as much for him as for her.

"I love you, April." He adjusted his position and added a second hand. She trembled harder, so close he could feel it. "Come for me, darlin'."

April came around him, biting her lip so as not to cry out, even though Clay was pretty sure the embarrassed nurse wouldn't be back for quite a while no matter what sounds came from his room.

He enjoyed every pulse of her body and when she finally calmed and lay breathless next to him, Clay was still hard and aching, but felt absolutely satisfied at the same time.

After far too many years April was back in his bed, something he had started to doubt would ever happen again.

Everything else could wait.

"Clay. I think maybe we should talk now."

Everything except, apparently, talking. "Okay, darlin'. I'm listening."

Chapter Sixteen

Mason awoke disoriented. His internal clock still messed up from traveling, being in an unfamiliar bed didn't help things any. But in spite of all that, he somehow felt rested. His body must have realized it could really sleep, that for the first time in months, he wouldn't be awoken by shouts of *Incoming*!

Realizing that if he wanted to see Clay he had to go inside the hospital now and also deal with being near April again, he decided he'd rather face mortar fire. At least that was exciting *and* he could fire back. Not so with the assault April waged on his heart. With her, he just had to sit helpless in the face of the pain.

Judging by the light outside, it was late in the morning. He'd gotten to bed so late, it was no wonder he'd slept so long. Swinging past the cafeteria, Mason picked up two cups of coffee and two danish, figuring they had to be better than whatever Clay would get fed for breakfast. He stifled the feeling of guilt for not getting anything for April. She used to drink tea, but who the hell knew what she liked now, certainly not cowboys, that was for sure.

Holding on tight to his bad mood all the way to Clay's room, Mason walked through the open door and breathed a sigh of relief. He was alone. Maybe she'd gone back to New York with Ben Ben, or taken an early train.

"Hey! I brought you some chow."

Clay's face lit up. "Thanks. You wouldn't believe what they brought me for breakfast. Green gelatin and some sort of rubbery eggs. What the hell kind of meal is that for a man who's trying to recover?"

Mason laid Clay's coffee, pastry and an assortment of sweeteners and creamers on his tray.

Clay picked up the Danish and bit into it with a groan. "Now *that* is a good breakfast."

Mason laughed, not so certain the doctors would agree, but at least his friend seemed happy, and after what he'd been through, he deserved it. "How are you feeling this morning?"

He looked better at least, lying on top of the sheets and dressed in sweats and a t-shirt rather than the hospital gown. And Clay had far more color in his cheeks than he'd had since Mason's arrival in Philly. In fact, he was almost glowing.

"I feel great! My sole goal is to prove to these doctors I'm strong enough to get the hell out of here. Hopefully today."

Mason raised a brow. "And then what?"

Clay returned his sharp look. "I know I can't jump right back into competition. Don't worry. I'll take a few days to work out the kinks on April Dawn in private before I go back."

A few days? Mason didn't need to speak with the specialists treating Clay to know they wouldn't approve of a few days of recuperation before he jumped up on a bucking bronc. "Well, you're gonna have to do it back in Oklahoma, cause that's where April Dawn is gonna be."

"What are talking about? Did they ship her back already? I thought you saw her last night."

"I did, and no, they didn't ship her back, but I will. I've got your trailer and I've made plans with the stockman to get her before the rodeo moves out. I'll be driving her back to the Carson's farm. I'm sure they'll be fine with that but I'll call and check anyway. You can catch a flight home when the doctor says it's okay and meet me there. We'll work out together and when the local docs say you're good to go, then you can get back into competition, and not before."

Clay watched him with a look of surprise. "You got this all figured out, don't you?"

Mason grinned. "Yeah. You got a problem with that?"

He could see Clay's brain working as he considered what Mason had told him. Finally, Clay returned his smile. "Nah. I'm good. But I do have a favor to ask you."

Mason nodded. "Anything you want. What is it?"

The sound of a shower running suddenly turned silent.

"Can I tell you later?"

Taking a big bite of his danish, Mason shrugged. "Sure."

Clay grinned and took a big sip of coffee. "Mmm, mmm. I think I love you, man."

Mason shook his head, laughing, until Clay's bathroom door opened and a wet-headed April emerged. Mason realized the shower he'd heard running wasn't in the neighboring room as he'd assumed.

The sugary breakfast didn't seem to be sitting as well as it had before April, dressed in some little top and pants that clung to her ass, stepped into the room. She halted for a second when she saw him, then went to her bag to put something away.

"Hey darlin'. Feel better?" Clay stretched one hand out to her.

She walked closer, squeezed it, then let it drop with a quick glance in Mason's direction. "Much better. Thank you,

Clay."

"Good, because I've got a surprise for you."

Mason watched April raise one brow prettily. He scowled at himself for noticing and looked away.

Clay continued. "I got you a ride back home to your parents' farm."

Mason whipped his head around to glare at Clay, wide-eyed, as April answered. "I still have to find out from my boss if I can take the time off."

"Go call now and ask him," Clay suggested.

She laughed. "I'm not certain he'll answer this early. He was up pretty late last night, I'm sure."

"So were you, but you're awake." Clay grinned.

Clay better get April out of there, because Mason had a few things to say to his *friend* once they were alone.

Finally, April nodded and fished her cell phone out of her huge bag. "Okay, I'll just go down to the lobby where the signal's better."

Good idea, Mason thought silently. April was barely out the door when Mason hissed, "Goddammit, Clay!"

Clay's response was a grin. "What?"

"You tricked me into that! There is no way I'm going to be trapped in a vehicle with her from here to Oklahoma and once you tell her about it, I'm sure she won't like it any more than I do. You can just fly her there if she wants to go home. With all the winning you do, you must have the money."

"Money's not the issue. She won't accept a plane ticket from me, I offered last night when she mentioned how much she missed home."

"Then ask her parents to buy her the plane ticket. Or, hell, buy it and pretend her parents paid for it. I don't care what you do, but I am not taking her."

"She wouldn't accept it. She's trying to be independent." Clay's eyes bore into Mason. "We had a long talk last night about a lot of things, but in particular, about the three of us."

"Well, that's real nice for you, but as far as I'm concerned, there is no *us*. That ended when she went to New York and stopped writing because we were no longer good enough for her."

The steady sway of Clay's head prompted Mason to ask sharply, "What?"

"There's more to it, Mason. She had her reasons…"

Mason cut him off. "And I don't want to hear them."

"You promised you'd do anything I asked."

"That's unfair, Clay. You didn't tell me it was *this*. I can't do it."

"You mean you won't do it."

"No, I mean I can't." Mason glanced at the still empty doorway and lowered his voice. "I can barely even look at her without feeling sick inside."

"Because you're still in love with her."

"The hell I am." Mason lied to Clay, but it wasn't so easy lying to himself.

"Mason. We've been through a lot together, and even though we've taken different paths the last few years, I still count you as my closest friend."

Damn, Clay was good at pulling on a person's heartstrings. "I know. Me too."

"Do you trust me?"

Mason sighed. Where was this leading? "Yes, of course I do."

"Then do me this one small favor like you promised."

He had promised to do Clay a favor, but Mason had never promised to do *this*. When he remained silent, his jaw clenched too tightly to speak, Clay added, "Please, Mason."

April walked in, halting one step inside the room as she glanced from Clay to Mason and back again. No way she could miss the heavy tension that hung between them. She looked so small and unsure, even dressed in her sophisticated New York clothes.

"Um, I explained things and even though he wasn't happy, my boss finally agreed that I could take a week off."

She gripped her phone in her hand tightly, like a child with her security blanket. Mason wasn't so sure she was all that keen about going home. It looked like Clay had been a busy boy the last twelve hours or so, orchestrating everybody's life, making them all do things they didn't want to do to suit himself.

"That's great, darlin'!" Clay looked pointedly at Mason, the question unspoken.

Mason did some quick estimations in his head. It had to be over a thousand miles from Philly to Oklahoma. Shit, that would mean about twenty-four straight hours alone with April, most of them spent in the close confines of the trailer cab with them stopping only often enough to care for April Dawn's and their own personal needs.

But Clay looked so damned happy, and April might be the one thing that would keep him recuperating at the farm rather than trying to jump right back into competition.

Shit. Mason let out a deep sigh. "Okay, Clay."

Clearly the victor in this battle, his friend grinned wide. "Great."

Mason scowled. *Great. Just great.*

Chapter Seventeen

April had to run to keep up with Mason's fast stride. She'd forgotten exactly how long his legs were, although in the past, she'd never had trouble keeping up with him, probably because back then, he slowed his pace to hers and wasn't trying to run away from her.

She didn't know how much more she could take of him treating her like this. She had to tell him about the miscarriage, but as she struggled to run in her heels to even keep him in view as he rounded the corner of the building, now was not the time. The ride home would be soon enough, and the sooner the better because a whole day and night on the road alone with him in this mood would really suck.

He'd reached the front entrance to the arena and turned to shoot her an impatient look as he waited for her to catch up.

"I'm sorry. I can't move that fast in these heels." April thought herself in pretty good shape from walking everywhere in the city, but maybe she wasn't since she was breathless now. "And why did you park all the way over there if the door is here?"

"I parked by the door nearest the stock pens inside. You've been to enough arenas with Clay and me to know the stock gets loaded around back."

That time in her life felt like a million years ago yet at the same time, she could still remember exactly how Mason's kisses felt.

Mason raised one brow, glancing down at her totally impractical shoes. "And why didn't you wait with the truck if you can't walk in those things?"

Good question. Looking at the annoyance on his face she had to ask herself the same thing. "Too late now. Let's just get this horse and get on the road."

"Fine with me." He pulled open the door and, surprisingly, didn't let it slam in her face, but instead held it open for her. At least that was something.

Inside the arena, Mason seemed to know his way around and was able to locate a stock contractor amid the hustle and bustle of the preparations for the rodeo to move out to the next venue.

177

He stalked directly to the stock and located what must be Clay's horse. "Hey there, baby girl. You ready to go home?"

April's heart twisted at the familiarity of the gentle tone of voice he used with the horse. The same tone he used to use with her. She didn't have long to wallow though, because a woman was leading a horse directly at her and April had to scurry to get out of the way. She missed getting stepped on, but did not miss the look the cowgirl shot her as she took April in from the tips of her impractical designer heels to the now horrendously wrinkled silk of her top.

The woman kept her mouth shut even while her eyebrows rose, but April was not the object of her attention for long. Mason, however, was. "Hey there, Mason sugar! I was hoping to see you again before I hauled ass out of here."

Mason nodded at the tart…um, cowgirl, and even smiled at her. "Hey, Kit. Is this your barrel horse?"

She nodded. "Yup. This here's Duke."

It seemed Mason had a kind word for this cleavage-baring woman but could barely speak civilly to her. April watched the exchange through narrowed eyes, denying that what she felt was jealousy.

"You need help loading April Dawn in the trailer, sugar?"

The horse's name cut through April's green haze of envy. "April Dawn?" she repeated softly.

That comment drew this Kit person's attention. "That's what Clay named her. And what's your name, sweetie? I'm Kit, a friend of Clay's."

A friend. Yeah, April bet she was! Her photo may have been found in Clay's jeans, but she bet Kit had been in his pants a few times herself.

She somehow managed to spew out her name. "April."

At that revelation, Kit raised an eyebrow and shot a look at Mason, who returned it with a slight nod. April's anger and jealousy ramped up another notch.

Mason ignored her totally and spoke to Kit. "Things are pretty crazy around here right now, so I don't know if I'll be able to find a stockman to help me load her up. So I sure would appreciate your help, if you've got the time."

April turned to Mason and frowned. "I can help you load her up."

He raised a brow and let his eyes drop down to her shoes again. "I don't think so. Kit can handle it."

Dammit. It wasn't like she had brought a lot of footwear options with her from New York and Mason knew it!

Out of the corner of her eye, April saw Kit grin. "Just let me load Duke, sugar, and I'll be right back to give you a hand."

"Thanks." Mason nodded in Kit's direction, then turned to April, looking amused at her expense. He fished the trailer

179

keys out of his pocket. "If you want to help, you can go out this door here and get the truck. Back it right up to the exit."

Grinding her teeth to keep from saying anything that would embarrass herself, April snatched the keys from his hand. "Fine."

April spun on her heel and had to do a little dance to sidestep a fresh steaming pile of manure deposited there by Kit's horse, Duke. Scowling, she avoided looking back at him as she heard Mason chuckle behind her and she realized it was very difficult to stomp away in high heels.

Clay sat on the front porch, an icy glass of sweet tea and a plate of fresh baked cookies the neighbor had brought over sat on the table next him, along with his very own little bell. *A bell!* In case he needed something while she was inside, his mother had told him. He sighed. Perhaps if it had been a big old cowbell instead of this delicate little tinkling thing it wouldn't have been quite so humiliating. At least she'd left him alone for a few minutes, but only so she could go in and start cooking his favorite dinner.

He'd only been off the plane from Philly for a few hours so he hoped she'd lighten up after a little time had passed. She would have to, because as soon as Mason and April arrived from Philly with his trailer he intended on moving back into his own home. No way was he sleeping in his parents' house while April was back in town, not when he had his own place, complete with a king sized bed and acres of privacy. Besides, he was in no shape to go crawling through April's bedroom window to be with her, though with all the painkillers he was on, it probably wouldn't hurt too much.

He heard the phone ringing inside the house, and his mama's voice answering it before the screen door slammed.

"That was Mrs. Carson. April called them from the road and said they'd be there within the quarter hour. Mason wants to unload April Dawn first, then he said to tell you he'd be over with the trailer."

"Can you drive me over to the Carson's place?" Clay wiggled his butt forward in the chair and gripped the arms, ready to stand.

"What? You just got out of the hospital. You can't be traipsing all over town."

"I won't be traipsing. You'll be driving me."

Clay's mother opened her mouth to protest when his father came out onto the porch. "The boy can sit at the Carson's just as well as he can sit here. I'll drive you, Clay. We'll be back by dinner, Marge. I promise. Come on, son. I'm sure you want to see that horse of yours."

With a sly wink, Clay's father told him he knew his son

was just as anxious to see April, as April Dawn.

He smiled. "Thanks, Pop."

Clay's heart beat faster the closer they got to the farm. When they pulled up the familiar drive and he saw Mason and April standing next to his trailer, his blood was absolutely pounding in his ears.

"Can you pull right over to the barn?"

"Sure thing, but don't tell your mother." His father grinned.

The closer they got, the more clear it became that the idea of getting April and Mason to make peace by trapping them in a vehicle together for a thousand miles hadn't worked as he planned.

It looked like April's father had taken April Dawn to the pasture to stretch her legs for a bit. Meanwhile, April's mother was just coming out of the kitchen door. She saw him in the car and waved with a smile.

With the car window open, Clay could clearly hear April as she spat at Mason, "Maybe you should have brought your girlfriend Kit with you instead of me."

Mason folded his arms across his chest. "She'd have been more helpful than you were in those ridiculous clothes. And not that it is any of your business, but she's not my girlfriend."

April mirrored his pose. "That's not what it looked like

when you kissed her goodbye."

Looking amused, Mason shook his head. "*She* kissed *me*. And what do you care? Are you jealous of her?"

"Jealous? Of her? Ha! Honestly, why did she bother wearing a shirt at all? It was buttoned so low I could practically see her whole bra!"

Mason's brows shot up. "At least she was wearing a bra, unlike you, in that dress you were wearing the other night!"

"That dress is a designer original."

"Yeah, so the designer told me himself. Figures a man would design a dress with no front."

"He's gay!"

"So he says."

April drew in a huge breath, about to lay into Mason again when Clay had had enough. Besides his annoyance with them both for still fighting, April's mama was now near enough to hear and he didn't want her to witness their fight. With a quick glance at his father, who looked more than interested in the exchange between Mason and April, Clay hoisted himself out of the car and stumbled forward, purposefully looking helpless and more wobbly than he really was. It worked, they forgot about fighting and both leapt forward to grab him.

"Jeez, Clay. You shouldn't be out." Mason held him by both arms.

"And you shouldn't be fighting," he hissed. Clay looked to April's mother. "Hello, Mrs. Carson. How are you?"

"How are you, is the more important question." She stepped forward and squeezed his hand warmly.

"I'm good. I'll be back in the saddle before you know it. And I wanted to thank you for keeping April Dawn here for a bit."

She dismissed him with a wave of her hand. "Don't be silly. She can stay as long as you need. And if there is anything else we can do for you, don't hesitate to ask."

"Thank you, ma'am. Actually, there is something you can do for me." Clay shot his father a meaningful glance. "Could you take my dad inside to call my mother and let her know we arrived all right? She's been a little protective about me lately."

Mrs. Carson let out a laugh. "I don't blame her one bit, honey. I would be, too. Come on, I'll show you the phone."

With one more interested glance, Clay's father followed Mrs. Carson inside and Clay, Mason, and April were alone, if only just for a moment.

He turned to them both. "I take it you two didn't talk about things during the trip."

April crossed her arms again and glared at Mason. "Every time I tried, he sneered at me and turned the radio louder."

Mason displayed that sneer now. "I told you. There is nothing to talk about."

"Fine. Then I'm going inside to shower and change. Hopefully, some of my old clothes are still here in my room. I've been in these, and in that truck with you, for far too long."

Clay watched her stalk away. "Mason…"

"Don't, Clay. You may be willing to forgive that she cut all ties with us in favor of her uppity New York friends, but I'm not."

"That's not how it was." Clay noticed April's father still busy with filling the water bucket in the far paddock for April Dawn and decided they still had a few minutes alone to work this out. "Mason…"

"Clay, I'm not gonna talk about it now. I have to go see my parents. Can I borrow the trailer?"

He stifled a sigh. "Of course. Will I see you again tonight?"

"Yeah. I can be back after dinner."

"Good. Um, I wanted to ask you something."

Glancing in the direction April had gone, Mason shook his head and laughed. "After I just unloaded this last favor, you're pushing your luck asking for another."

"It's not like the last one. I wanna sleep in my own house tonight. I'm there little enough as it is with all the travel, and I know my mother will never let me stay there alone. I've got a nice open-up sofa bed…"

Mason raised a brow. "You're asking me to stay there with you?"

Clay nodded.

"And you think staying there instead of sleeping in the too short twin sized bed in my old room with the cowboy wallpaper will be a favor for you?" Mason laughed.

Clay grinned at the image. "I sure would appreciate it. Besides, I want you to see my place. It's not much, just a small old farmhouse. But the barn is big and solid and once I have the time to rebuild the stalls and fence in a few more paddocks, it'll be perfect for me to retire there."

Mason laughed.

"What's so funny?"

"You. Talking about retiring already."

"You see many riders over forty?"

"Yeah, in the senior rodeo." Mason grinned.

"Exactly." Clay leaned on the fence post as his pain medication began to wear off and the aches in his back and neck made him feel more like seventy than twenty-something. "I figure I've got fifteen years left max, and that's barring a career-ending injury. When the farm went up for sale, I thought it was best to grab it. The down payment emptied out my savings account pretty good but I didn't know if such a good opportunity would ever come up again. I think I can make a go of training rough stock there."

"You sure do have a knack for it. The stock contractor couldn't say enough about April Dawn."

"Yeah. I know." Clay kicked at the dirt. "So, will you stay with me and save me from having my mother tuck me into my old twin sized bed tonight?"

"Yeah, no problem. Besides, I've been wanting to see your place ever since you wrote me about buying it."

Clay slapped him on the back, wincing as his sore muscles protested the motion. "Great!"

One down, one to go.

As Mason drove away with a promise to meet Clay at his place later, Clay made his way slowly to the house, hoping the entire achy way that some of the clothes still left in April's old room included her tiny cut-off denim shorts and her old cowboy boots. With that tempting image fueling his progress, he almost forgot he needed his painkillers.

Chapter Eighteen

A little while after eating dinner with his parents, Mason made his excuses and headed for Clay's farm. He loved his mother and father, but years spent living apart from home meant that a little teary-eyed fawning by them went a long way. Besides, he'd be there for a month. They had plenty of time to spend together.

More than ready to kick back in peace and quiet with his friend and a beer, Mason drove up Clay's drive, glad it was still just light enough that he could get his first glimpse of the property and the outside of the house.

Clay'd done good. The place needed a little work, but it had some good bones to build upon.

Mason sprinted up the front steps and through the screen door, not bothering to knock since he didn't want Clay to try and get up to answer the door, then he came to a halt.

April sat on the couch next to Clay. The couch where Clay had said he could sleep tonight. And as Mason realized that was probably Clay's plan all along, his eyes narrowed in on his supposed friend.

"Clay…" Mason's voice was almost a low growl.

Clay interrupted his protest. "April didn't want me to be all alone until you arrived. Besides, I thought we could all talk."

"We've done all the talking we need to."

Mason watched April cross her arms defiantly. "He's right, Clay. Let it go."

At least he and April agreed on one thing.

Clay, however, didn't. "No. I won't. And if you won't tell him, April, I will."

Mason watched April's eyes open wide as she turned to Clay. "Clay. No!"

Clay's gaze moved from April to Mason as he said, "I'm sorry, darlin'. But it has to be said."

Her voice came out in a whisper. "Clay. Please."

Wasn't this interesting. There was something April didn't want him to know. Now Mason was intrigued. Mason crossed his own arms and waited. He didn't have to wait long.

Clay took April's hand in his but his eyes were trained

on Mason, where he still stood by the door. "She got pregnant that summer, Mason."

The blood rushing through Mason's ears at that revelation made it nearly impossible for him to hear what Clay said next.

"And before you get angry that she kept it to herself all that time, she didn't know about it 'til after she got to New York and by then it was too late."

Ignoring the tears in April's eyes, Mason swallowed and asked Clay, "What do you mean *too late*?"

"She lost the baby and that freaked her out pretty bad." Clay squeezed her hand. "That's why she stopped writing and calling us."

Mason looked between the two of them. "How long have you known?" he accused Clay.

April finally spoke, answering his question. "I told Clay in the hospital. I tried to tell you a ton of times, but…"

"I wouldn't let you." Mason took a deep breath. "I need some air."

They didn't try to stop him when he stalked out the door and into the cool night. He didn't stop himself until he'd reached the barn, where he slumped against the wall and covered his face with his hands.

There'd almost been a baby. *His* baby most likely. He was fairly sure of that as he remembered the night in the lake, their first time together when he'd barely pulled out in time.

He let out a laugh. Obviously he *hadn't* pulled out in time at all.

Soft footsteps told him he was no longer alone.

"You okay?"

Imagine that, April asking him if he was all right when she was the one who'd been pregnant. Was he okay? Good question. After a moment, he let out a shaky breath. "Yeah."

April stood before him looking so young and unsure. With a sigh, Mason looped one forearm around her neck and pulled her to him. She sighed against him.

"April. What would you have done? If you didn't lose it, I mean."

"I honestly don't know."

"I would have married you, you know."

He felt her laugh reverberate through his chest where her head rested against him. It scared him how good it felt to have her there again.

"Oh, yeah, because you really wanted to be married with a baby at eighteen years old while you were in boot camp." Her voice dripped in sarcasm.

"You don't know that." He let out a sad laugh. "It doesn't matter, you wouldn't have wanted to marry a mediocre amateur rodeo cowboy turned Army grunt anyway."

"You don't know that," she said softly.

His heart twisted at those words. He looked down at her, as much as he could see in the fading light of dusk. "I really did love you, you know."

She stared up at him for a moment. Her eyes never left his face as she said, "And I loved you."

Mason let out a deep sigh and said the one thing he never thought he'd ever say again to this woman. "I still do."

He heard her sharp intake of breath before she answered, "So do I."

Her mouth was against his then, though which one of them moved first, he couldn't judge. It didn't matter once his lips met hers and her body sank deeper against his.

The feel of her hair, the taste of her mouth, the smell of her skin, it was like coming home. The years melted away and the hurt faded until Mason's world narrowed to just his mouth on hers.

Mason reversed their positions until she was crushed between his body and the barn. He groaned at the warmth of her tongue against his. It would be so easy, so natural, to sink into her warm body right there where they stood. If they were both eighteen again, he had no doubt they would have given in to their frantic need right then and there. But a few years of living had put some perspective on that crazy summer.

With her face clutched in both hands he pulled away and leaned his forehead against hers. "And Clay?"

"Nothing's changed, Mason."

"You still love him." It wasn't a question. The fact she'd driven from New York in the middle of the night with not much more than the clothes on her back when she'd heard he'd been hurt had already told him that.

She nodded. "Yes, I do. Mason, the three of us made it work before…"

He shook his head. "We were kids before, and it worked for all of two months."

"I'd rather die than lose either one of you. I can't…I won't choose between the two of you. I couldn't then, I won't now."

Mason sighed. Could they do this again? He'd be going back to Germany after his leave and April would be gone at the end of the week. Maybe he shouldn't try to think past that point and just enjoy the here and now. If he'd learned anything in the Army it had been that. "Okay."

He felt her startle at his answer. "Really?"

His cock hardened just at the thought of the three of them in Clay's bed with no parents in the house to worry about walking in on them. Mason laughed, surprised at himself. "Yeah."

April took a shaky breath. "Can we go inside now?"

The sooner the better. "Yeah. Sure."

The look on Clay's face when Mason and April walked into the living room holding hands was a comical cross of shock and pure glee. "You made up."

Still a little annoyed at Clay's interfering, Mason nodded and pulled April toward the back of the house. "Yup. We did. I'm assuming the bedroom's in this direction so we're gonna head on back now and get reacquainted, if you know what I mean."

April looked up at him with wide-eyed horror at his announcement as her cheeks reddened. She had always been ridiculously easy to embarrass.

Clay's smile turned into a frown. "Hey!"

Mason raised a brow. "You coming or not?"

"Hell yeah, I'm coming." Clay pulled himself stiffly forward on the couch cushion.

April smacked Mason's arm and extracted her hand from his. "Mason, go help him off the couch and stop teasing."

"Alright." Mason gave Clay a hand up and whispered, "But don't think I'm helping you fuck. There you're on your own. Got it?"

Clay grinned wide. "*That* I'll manage, even if it kills me."

Mason watched April's jean clad ass heading for the

bedroom. Was it rounder than it used to be? Were those faded jeans she'd salvaged from her old room in her parents' house just a tad tight now? He shook his head, practically salivating. "It just may kill us both."

Once April had disappeared into the other room, Mason turned serious. "Why didn't you let me stay angry and keep her for yourself? I would have gone back after my leave and you could have had a happy ever after, just the two of you."

Clay pressed his lips together in thought before he answered. "When April and I had that talk in the hospital, I realized half of her would always belong to you, whether you two were together or apart. I want her, yeah, but I want her to be whole, not torn in half."

Mason laughed at how dead on Clay could be when it came to reading people sometimes, the same way he could always read horses. "When did you turn into the philosopher?"

"I guess laying under eleven hundred pounds of floundering horseflesh makes you take stock of things." Clay shrugged.

Mason nodded. "I guess it would." So did facing death each day in the Afghan desert, only Mason had still let his anger and hurt rule him for the past few years when it came to April. No more.

He turned toward the bedroom when Clay held him back

with a hand on his arm "You really okay with this?"

Mason took a second to answer. "Yeah. I am."

Clay watched him closely. "You don't sound so sure."

"No, I am. It's just…" He shook his head. He never had and never would admit this to another living person, but this was Clay, and for better or worse, they were in this thing together. "Maybe if I didn't get hard enough to hammer nails at the thought of sharing her with you I would feel better about the whole thing. What's with that? It can't be normal, you know? Getting excited over watching your best friend with your girl."

"I don't know what's normal anymore and what's not. I just know that the three of us together, it's…" Clay laughed. "I can't describe it."

Mason nodded. He couldn't find the words to describe it either. "Come on. April's waiting."

The moment Clay saw April laid out naked on his bed, thoughts of what he wanted to do to her replaced the awareness of the bone-deep ache in his back.

"Pretty confident, were we?" Mason said next to him, nodding his head in the direction of the nightstand where a box of condoms and a bottle of lube sat.

Clay raised a brow at April. "That's not mine, but I'm

sure glad it's there."

Mason shot him a surprised glance, which then shifted to April.

"I bought them," she confirmed, blushing prettily. "I borrowed the car and went to the store in town. I told my parents I needed to pick up some things."

Clay flashed back to the memory of him and Mason at eighteen, driving more than half an hour to a store three towns away so no one they recognized would see them buying condoms. Meanwhile, April waltzed right into town to make the purchase.

This was a whole new April. She may still blush, but she also bought her own condoms. Clay liked the change. He moved toward the bed and raised a knee to crawl onto the mattress, heading for his favorite spot between April's legs, when his injuries made themselves known again. There was no hiding his cringe.

A naked April sat up in concern. "Clay! You're in pain. I can see it on your face. You need to lie down and take it easy."

Mason shot him a look of concern as Clay snorted out a laugh. "Not much chance of that, darlin'."

April smiled. "I don't mean that we can't…you know."

Clay grinned that after all these years she still couldn't talk about sex out loud.

"I meant you should lie flat on your back and let me...us...do all the work," she continued, glancing at Mason.

Clay raised a brow in amusement at that offer. "Okay. I guess I can do that." His cock sure liked the idea. It stood right up and took notice in his jeans at the thought of April riding him while he did nothing but enjoyed it.

"I'll get you a pain pill." She started to rise but he held up one hand.

"Not yet, darlin'. It's been too long since we've done this and I don't anything blocking what I feel. I can deal for a little while."

She looked skeptical, but nodded.

Moments later Clay didn't think again about pain or pills. Boots and clothes were in two heaps on the floor where he and Mason had let them drop where they stood, and April was above him, her mouth on his, her hand wrapped around his long-neglected erection, her ass in the air with her legs spread wide as her knees straddled him.

Clay felt her catch her breath as Mason kneeled behind her and began using both his hands and mouth on her. She groaned and shivered as Mason did something she particularly liked, and Clay got, if possible, harder in her grasp. He grabbed her hair in one fist, angled his mouth over hers and plunged his tongue into her.

He was aware of Mason's weight shifting on the mattress, heard him snap open the bottle of lube and seconds later, felt April arch her back with a gasp. Now it was Clay's turn to shiver as he imagined, no, *knew*, that Mason had slid a slick finger into April's ass. Mason had eventually figured out how much she liked it that summer, and it was obvious now that she was still as responsive and sensitive as ever. He felt her rocking back against Mason, seeking more.

Clay heard another squirt of lube right before April let out a gasp and a moan. *Two fingers now*, he thought. He could practically feel what Mason felt as April's body opened in response to his probing fingers. They'd done this dance before, the three of them. He didn't even need to look to know what Mason was doing to her. As she began to shake, Clay thought, *Close. She'll come soon.*

Mason felt it too because he said, "Cover Clay, baby."

She nodded, breathless, and rolled a condom over him with shaking hands. But when she braced herself on shaky arms on either side of him and moved to slide him inside, Mason held her hips back and told her in a gravelly voice, "Not yet."

Clay heard one more squirt of lube and saw Mason move up close behind April while his fingers came back around and began to circle her clit. It had always been easier to slide into her ass if she was on the verge of an orgasm.

As her breaths began to come in gasps, Clay watched April's eyes squeeze tightly shut as Mason, whose own eyes closed in response to the sensation Clay knew well, pressed his lubed cock inside her. He knew exactly what Mason felt as he pushed in slowly, fighting the initial tightness of her muscles, sliding deeper as her body relaxed and accepted him. He'd been there himself many times. But what he suspected was about to come next they'd never done together.

Fully seated inside her, Mason's hands on her hips guided her forward, positioning April's entrance over Clay. "Now, baby."

Clay had trouble breathing as she slid down over his quivering length. Her pussy felt tighter than ever, thanks to Mason already filling her ass. In all their times together, she'd never taken them both at once like this. Clay somehow managed to open his eyes and ask, "You okay, darlin'?"

She swallowed hard and nodded. "Yeah." He felt her insides quiver around him.

"Can Mason move inside you? Cause I can't." Besides his back, which he seemed to have forgotten for a bit while lost in the moment, he had April's full weight plus that of Mason pressing into her, pinning him to the mattress.

She nodded and, eyes closed, dropped her head forward over him as Mason starting moving slowly in and out of her.

Beneath the veil of April's hair falling around him, Clay's breath caught in his throat. Every one of Mason's strokes rubbed against Clay's cock. He hadn't anticipated that he'd be able to feel Mason inside her. It probably would have freaked him out a bit if he had more time to think about it. But he didn't because April, grinding her hips against him as she sought to bring on her own orgasm, started to come. Then all he felt or cared about was her muscles gripping him, milking him. Both he and Mason gasped at the same time as they shared the sensation.

Clay forced his eyes open to watch April's face when she came with her eyelids squeezed tightly shut as she bit her lower lip.

She whimpered softly in her throat, a sound familiar to them both from that one summer they had together. Only this time, unlike then, her parents weren't in the house. This time, there was no risk of awakening them. "Don't hold back, darlin'. There's no one to hear you but us."

At that, Mason groaned and thrust faster and April came harder and louder than ever before.

Clay didn't hold back. Why should he? They had all night and he was long overdue. Shouting, he let himself come with long, hard spurts inside April amid the combined sensations of her throbbing and Mason thrusting. And somehow it all felt perfectly natural to him and he knew deep down, this was how they were meant to be.

Chapter Nineteen

Mason stared out the kitchen window at the reddened sky as he sipped good, strong, scalding hot coffee from one of Clay's mugs. After chow hall coffee and most recently hospital vending machine brew, it had been far too long since he'd had a decent cup. Lucky for them all, Clay's mother had only agreed to let Clay stay in the house if he let her stock the kitchen and if Mason did him the favor of staying there with him. Little did she know sleeping here was no favor and no hardship.

"Morning." Clay, sun-bleached hair sticking up all over, stumbled half asleep into the kitchen, one hand rubbing his lower back.

"Morning. You feeling okay?"

"I think I'd rather have broken bones than this soft tissue

injury crap. I woke up real stiff." Clay laughed as his inadvertent joke registered and added, "In many places. April's still sleeping or I might have been tempted to stay in bed myself."

Mason smiled. Yeah, waking up in bed with April was enough to make any man stiff and tempted, himself no exception. "You need a pain pill for your back?"

"In a bit. I'll take a cup of that coffee now though." Clay pulled out a kitchen chair and sat heavily.

"You got it." Mason poured him a steaming cup and paused. "I don't know how you take your coffee." After what they'd done the night before, that fact struck him as totally ridiculous.

Clay shook his head and then winced as his neck must have reminded him his pills had worn off. "Just a spoon of sugar, and don't beat yourself up over it. I didn't drink coffee back when we were eighteen. Neither did you. I guess it's a habit that comes with age."

"Yeah, I guess it is." Mason glanced out the window again. Now that it was daylight, he got a nice view of Clay's property. "The barn and the fields look good. A little work and this place will be perfect."

Clay laughed. "Yeah, if I had the time to do it myself, or the money to hire out the work, it sure could. As it is, I don't have enough of either at the moment to get the job done."

Mason turned to him. "I could do some of it for you while I'm here. I've got a month leave."

"I can't have you working while I sit here and watch."

"You're hurt, and I'm used to work. I'll go nuts here with nothing to do." *Especially when April leaves again for New York in less than a week.*

Clay hesitated then finally agreed. "Okay. Maybe if you just strung the fencing in the new paddock. I already sank the posts. I like to be able to rotate the field where I turn April Dawn out."

"You want me to go get her today from the Carson's and bring her back here?"

"I left her there not only because I wasn't sure I'd be able to take care of her by myself, but because I've got no feed and no hay here. And I need a delivery of bedding and to clean out her stall… I can't do all that right now."

"But you're not by yourself. I'm here. Besides, it will be good to be around horses again."

Clay grinned. "Okay. Since you're bound and determined to make me indebted to you, I'll let you muck my stalls and unload my feed and hay, too. Happy?"

"Yes." Actually, Mason was. Some hard physical labor might take his mind off the pointlessness of starting this thing up between the three of them again when it was destined to end with them all apart. Which was actually probably for the best, because how the hell could the three of them all live together without people eventually noticing something was off?

Speaking of noticing something… Mason tilted his head in the direction of the bedroom. "What do you think her parents are going to say that she spent the night here in the house with the two of us?"

Clay laughed. "Still worried about Mr. Carson's shotgun, are you?"

Mason had faced worse than that but, yeah, he was. He wasn't stupid. "Mess with a man's daughter and pay the consequences."

"She told them she'd be spending the night on the couch in case you needed help nursing me during the night." Clay waggled his eyebrows.

"I thought I was supposed to sleep on the couch," Mason reminded him.

"You slept in the chair, because that is the kind of dedicated friend you are." Clay grinned at him.

Mason shook his head. "You think you got it all figured out, don't you?"

"For now I do. We'll work on the rest later."

"Work out what later?" April wandered into the kitchen silently on bare feet, wearing an oversized t-shirt he recognized from the old days and looking worlds away from the girl in the red dress who had appeared at the hospital that night.

"How to get the rest of the fencing up for the other paddocks, that's what," Clay lied smoothly. "Get yourself together, darlin', because after breakfast we're heading over to your parents' farm."

She frowned sleepily. "Why?"

"I want to tell your daddy when we'll be collecting April Dawn."

Mason shook his head, hoping that was all they collected from April's daddy.

Clay continued, "And I want to see if Mason can still sit a horse after all this time."

That brought Mason's gaze around. "What?"

"April Dawn needs to be worked out. I can't do it and I can't think of a better man for the job than you."

Mason groaned. Clay was still up to something. Probably hoping that once he got up on a horse he'd forget all about his Army career.

A tiny song began to sound from the other room and April dove through the doorway to grab her bag. "That's my boss' ringtone."

Mason watched her through the open door. Little did Clay know, the only incentive Mason needed to not re-up, to come back here and trade his combat boots for cowboy boots, was April and the fact she still affected him like a drug he couldn't get enough of. But as she nodded her head vigorously and placated her boss with promises of returning to New York by the end of the week, Mason figured that, like all drugs, it would have been best if he'd just said no. Too bad it was too late for that now.

April finally disconnected the call and came back into the kitchen, looking frazzled.

Clay looked concerned. "Everything okay, darlin'?"

She took a deep breath and nodded. "Yeah. Just some work stuff."

Mason didn't like the look on her face, and liked her boss even less for putting it there. He stepped closer to April, pulled her to him and planted a hot full-out kiss on her mouth. When he pulled away, her eyes drifted open slowly and he saw the heat in them. "How about we postpone breakfast and the trip to your parents' for a bit and head back to bed?"

April blushed as Clay grinned. "I like how you think, my friend."

Being around horses again, not to mention at the Carson's farm where so much of his youth had been spent, felt surreal. But no more so than when two lanky kids came around the corner of the barn, one dark haired, one light-haired, both dressed in worn boots and jeans and sporting cowboy hats that had seen better days.

The sight stopped Mason in his tracks. Next to him, Clay laughed. "Yeah. Brings back memories, doesn't it?"

It sure as hell did. These two could have been he and Clay when they started working for Mr. Carson at thirteen, when they were clumsy kids still trying to navigate their pubescent bodies. Mason remembered that summer well. They couldn't get enough to eat they were shooting up so fast, and their mothers often bemoaned how fast they outgrew clothes. That had been the year they first became friends with April, the three of them inseparable by summer's end.

"It's going to suck when she's gone."

Mason's sobering observation wiped the cheerful look right off Clay's face. "Then let's not let her go."

Mason frowned and glanced sideways at his friend. "What do you suggest we do? Tie her up in the barn?"

Though the kinky side of him liked that idea for a short-term bit of fun, it was no way a long-term solution to the problem.

Clay grinned. "I haven't figured that out yet, but I like your idea about the barn."

Mason shook his head and sighed. "I guess it doesn't

matter. I'll be back in Germany in a few weeks anyway."

"Shouldn't you be just about done with your tour of duty, or whatever it's called?"

"Yeah, my contract is almost up. This one, anyway, until I reenlist."

"But you haven't reenlisted yet?"

"No. Not yet." He had planned to do it before he left Afghanistan, but then Clay had been injured and he'd left for home without another thought.

Mason could see the wheels in Clay's head turning.

Clay grinned. "Good."

"Why? Clay, what would I do here? I'm not a good enough rider to rank in the top ten the way you do. I'm a soldier now, and happy that I'm a good one."

"You're a cowboy first and always will be. It's in your blood, just like it's in mine."

Mason rolled his eyes. "So, what? I'll just follow you around and carry your saddle for you on the circuit like some roadie?"

"No, that's not what I'm suggesting. Look, Mason, if I ever want to get my farm in shape, and keep it running smoothly, I'm gonna need full-time help."

Mason rolled his eyes at Clay's attempt to get him to stay. "You already said you can't afford to pay someone to do that right now. And as crappy as my pay is in the Army, it's still better than getting paid nothing to muck your stalls."

"I'm not talking about hiring you. I'm talking about a partnership."

"A partnership in what?"

"Stock trainers. You and I. I choose the green horses at auction and train them when I'm not riding on the circuit. I can come home between rodeos. You run the farm and work with the stock when I'm traveling. At first we can just train and sell the broncs, at a huge profit, of course. Then, after I retire from competition, we can consider becoming contractors. Instead of selling, we supply the rough stock for the competitions."

Mason pictured a life where he could wake up each morning to good hot coffee and watch the sun rise over Clay's barn after sleeping soundly each night, the kind of sleep you could only get on a farm after a hard day's work. A life around both the horses and the rodeo he loved without having to get thrown in the dirt and depend on winning for his livelihood. Possibly a life that had some sort of a relationship with April in it, even a long distance one. At least they'd be on the same continent with him in Oklahoma.

Mason shook the images from his head. "You're crazy, Clay."

So why was he tempted? More than tempted, actually.

"Yeah, I've been called that before. But that's neither

here nor there. It's a good idea. You should see what I've been offered for April Dawn. We could make good money doing what we love. Just think about it. Okay?"

Mason drew in a deep breath, frightened at how good it all sounded. "Okay, I'll think about it, but what the hell does it matter? She's still going back to New York."

"I'm working on that."

He narrowed his eyes at his friend. "You're up to something again, aren't you?"

Clay just grinned. "Don't you worry. Now let's get these two kids to bring April Dawn on over and we'll see if you still remember how to ride."

Mason let out a long patient breath. "All right. But if I end up in a body cast because of you, you'll have my commanding officer to deal with."

Clay shrugged. "As if a mere man could scare me after I've faced El Diablo and lived to tell about it! Come on. No more procrastinating. Throw on a vest and let's get you back in the saddle."

Chapter Twenty

April had never felt so conflicted in her life. She loved both Clay and Mason. But Mason was going back to the Army, Clay was going back on the road, and she would be damned before she would sit at home like the little woman waiting for them to come home. So she would leave the men she loved to go back to her life in New York, and she was totally miserable about it as the number of days until she left grew shorter.

Standing next to the fence and watching Mason in the saddle had taken her back a few too many years. She might as well have been eighteen again, so in love she'd do anything.

The two men who held her heart captive stood talking now with two young boys watching them wide-eyed. Her dad had told her how the two kids he'd just hired worshipped Clay. What kids wouldn't? He'd started out just like them, mucking stalls for her daddy after school, and now he was one of the top ranking riders in the country.

April smiled and watched them listening with rapt attention as Clay explained something to Mason. She'd been inside with her mother visiting for a bit, but suddenly she needed to be closer to them. Her time here was so short, she didn't want even this small distance separating them. She moved closer and Clay smiled, looping an arm around her as he kept speaking with Mason.

"I think I know what's wrong."

Mason frowned. "What do you mean, what's wrong? I stayed on her, didn't I?"

"Yeah, but it wasn't pretty."

Mason scowled. "Hey, give me a break. I've been riding humvees the past few years, not horses."

Clay laughed. "Yeah, I know. But I've been thinking about it, how you used to ride when we were in competitions together. I don't know why I didn't see it then but it's clear as day now."

"What's clear?"

"Your style, the way you ride…you'd be better riding bareback than on a saddle bronc."

Mason rolled his eyes. "Bareback?"

Clay nodded. "Yeah, listen to me. You use more muscle, you try to overpower the bronc. That technique works better for bull riding or bareback bronc. Saddle bronc takes more timing, feeling the cadence of the horse, going with it, not fighting it."

"Like how you ride," Mason added.

Clay nodded and Mason took in a deep breath. "So how do I learn to do that?"

"You don't." Clay turned to the two boys, who were acting like they were witnessing history in the making. "Take her saddle off and change up her riggin', then load her into the chute again. We're gonna see how Mason does bareback," Clay instructed.

Shaking his head, Mason pushed his hat back off his forehead. "April Dawn's a saddle bronc."

"She could have gone either way when I bought her. I worked her out a few times bareback just to see. She'll be all right."

Mason shook his head. "God help you if you're wrong, Clay."

Clay glanced down at April and then back to Mason. "Have I been wrong so far?"

Mason let out a wry laugh. "Oh, shut up. No one likes a know-it-all."

Clay laughed and squeezed her closer to him, not

knowing that every moment spent in their presence squeezed her heart a little more.

She'd be fine once she was back home, in her apartment, busy at work and with Ben to hold her hand and make her feel better. That's what she needed. To talk to Ben. April watched Mason's ride, and just as Clay had predicted, he did great. She left them to discuss techniques and walked away.

"Tell me what to do," she said into her cell phone when Ben answered.

"Hmm. Let's see. You're in Oklahoma with two sexy as hell cowboys on a horse farm. I'll tell you what to do. That's an easy one. Ride those two cowboys until none of you can walk."

"Ben!"

"What? I'm serious."

She felt her cheeks grow hot. They'd already been doing that and now she was more confused than ever. "I mean, how can I leave them? What am I going to do at the end of the week when I'm supposed to fly back to New York?"

"Are you crazy? I wouldn't leave those two to come back here to that job and that one room joke you call an apartment."

"I love my job," she defended. She'd give in and let the apartment jab slide.

Ben snorted.

216

"What was that for?"

"I know better. You do *not* love your job. This is me you're talking to, remember. The one you bitch to when Christian works you to the bone, doesn't pay you what you deserve, yells at you when he's mad at someone else... Shall I go on?"

"No." April sighed. She knew he was right. She liked the idea of working for a Broadway director better than the reality of it. "But what do I do about my apartment?"

"When is your lease up?"

"Um, it expired last year and I never got around to renewing it."

Ben let out another sound of disgust. "Good. Then just move out. For what that landlord charges you for what I doubt is a legal apartment, but more likely half of the apartment next door that he added a wall to, he doesn't deserve notice and I'm sure he won't try making any trouble for you."

"But Mason is going back to the Army."

"Correct me if I'm wrong, but the Army isn't a life sentence, is it? They do let you out eventually."

"Yeah. I guess. But that doesn't mean Mason wants to get out."

"If you were living there again, I bet he wouldn't be able to get out fast enough."

"But Clay will be on the road riding a lot of the time."

Ben's voice sounded wearily indulgent. "And he'll be home when he's not."

April sighed. "This was exactly what I was afraid of. That the minute I saw them again I'd give up on my dreams and settle."

She could practically hear Ben's disagreement in his silence on the other end of the phone.

"Tell me what you're thinking, Ben."

"That if I had even one man who loved me the way those two love you I'd run to him, wherever the hell he lived. It's not *settling*. It's called being happy."

"But what about my career?"

"Let me ask you this, April. When you were a little girl and dreamed of your perfect job, what was it? Was it running after a self-centered diva after you picked up his dry cleaning and coffee, or did you have higher aspirations than that?"

April scowled at Ben's fairly accurate description of her current job. "I always wanted to be a reporter."

"Hmm. Correct me if I'm wrong, but there are newspapers, magazines, and TV stations even, elsewhere, other than Manhattan. Yes? Maybe even a few in the state of Oklahoma?"

April sighed, loving Ben more than ever, but hating how

he was persistently right all the time. "Yes."

"Any other arguments you can create to get in the way of your happiness or are you willing to give in and let those two hotties love you?"

That was a question April would have to think more about.

Mason found himself in Clay's kitchen again, staring out into the dusk. It had been an eye-opening day. He'd learned a few things. One, he was a pretty damn good bareback bronc rider. Two, Clay was eerily good at reading both horses and riders. Mason was actually starting to believe he…they…could make a success as stock trainers.

"What are you thinking about?"

Mason turned to find Clay leaning against the doorframe.

"How much I hate you right about now."

Clay raised a brow. "Oh?"

"Just when I thought I had my life figured out, you come back into it and turn it all upside down again. Bareback riding. April. Stock training. Quitting my Army career. Anything else you want to throw at me while you're at it?"

Clay grinned. "Nah, that about covers it for now. So what's the problem?"

"For one, April is leaving in a few days."

"I told you, I'm working on that."

Mason had no doubt. "Okay, let's say you pull off that miracle and convince her to stay. Then what? We live like some Mormon family?"

"Mormons have multiple wives, not husbands."

"See! We wouldn't even have an established religion to hide behind."

"Mason, look…" Clay looked out the window behind Mason and frowned. "What's my father doing here?"

Uh oh. Fathers didn't visit alone and at dinnertime unless something was up.

Shit. Mason pushed off the counter. "I'll get the door."

A moment later, back in the kitchen again, he and Clay faced Mr. Harris.

"Mason. Clay. I want to talk to you two."

Fathers also didn't start a conversation with those words unless someone was in trouble.

Clay nodded. "Sure thing. What's up?"

He glanced around. "Where's April?"

"She's having dinner at her parents' house. She'll be over later."

Mr. Harris raised a brow at that and took a deep breath before saying, "I'm pretty sure I know what's going on here."

Clay frowned, confused but Mason knew exactly what Clay's father thought he knew, and he was right. The man was observant, and there had been a lot to observe back in the hospital with Mason angry, April worried, and Clay thankful to be alive. Not to mention the big fight he'd witnessed after they'd arrived at the Carson's with the trailer. The three of them hadn't been too discreet lately at all.

"What are you talking about, Pop?"

"You two and April."

Realization dawned on Clay's face before he hid it. "I don't know what you're talking about. Want some coffee? I was just about to make some."

Mason bit one lip, thinking coffee wasn't going to distract Clay's father. Not when this was the topic of conversation.

Mr. Harris ignored Clay's attempt to change the subject and went on. "I can understand how it all happened. I always wondered back when you were in school what was going to happen if she ever chose one of you over the other. I guess the answer was she didn't choose, did she? Don't bother denying it because it's become pretty obvious to anyone who is looking that you two are both with her."

Clay remained shocked into silence as Mason kept his head down and his eyes focused on a crack in a tile on the

221

kitchen floor. Their lack of denial only proved Mr. Harris right as he continued. "I guess what I want to know is what you're going to do about it now?"

And that was one of Mason's main problems with this situation. The one he couldn't get over. They could live happily, just the three of them, but they didn't live in a bubble. Assholes like Clinton in the past, or even those who loved them, like Clay's father now, would always judge them. There'd be talk. He could take it. Clay probably could too, but April? It would destroy her.

At least it was Clay's father who confronted them now, and not someone else.

Clay straightened his spine. "I won't lose either one of them. Mason is my best friend and April is the woman I love."

His father took a deep breath. "I figured you'd say that. All right, then."

Mason raised a brow as Clay repeated, "All right?"

Mr. Harris shrugged. "What can I say? I love you, son, and I want you happy. And if this, as strange as it seems, makes you happy, then so be it."

Clay hugged his father before saying, "Um, Dad?"

"Yeah, son?"

"Does Mom know?"

"Not yet, no."

"What about the Carsons?" Clay asked his father.

"Not that I know of, but you'll have to tell them eventually. Your parents too, Mason. But I wouldn't tell the rest of the town. I'd keep it hidden if I were you. There'll be those who won't understand."

Mason finally couldn't remain silent any longer. "How do you suggest we do that? Keep people from knowing?"

"I've think I've got that figured out. To the public, it's gonna have to be like this. Clay and April are dating, and Mason is living here to manage the farm." Mr. Harris glanced at him. "Sorry, Mason. But it wouldn't seem right for you and your girlfriend to move in here together since it's Clay's place. It makes more sense if she's Clay's girl."

"It's fine, sir. Good, actually." Apparently scheming was a genetic trait among the Harris males. It might work, for a while at least. Eventually people might start to question why Mason never dated, though hopefully they'd just assume he was discreet.

Clay hugged his father again. "Thanks, Pop."

Mr. Harris shook his head. "Don't thank me. Just do me a favor. Let me lay some groundwork before we break this to your mother…"

"You think she'll be okay with it?" Clay asked.

His father nodded. "I think she will. All she wants is for you to be happy and anybody can see you are that."

When they were alone again, Mason shook his head at Clay. "This doesn't change a thing."

"Sure it does. One of the big issues you had with this was how others would view it. My father is fine with it."

"It doesn't change the fact that April will be leaving for New York."

He grinned. "We'll see."

After the surprise confrontation with Mr. Harris, Mason's nerves had had about enough. "What do you mean, we'll see?"

Clay smiled at him. "I think you'll find out in just a minute, because April just pulled up and she looks pretty happy."

As if on cue, April came flying into the kitchen. "I got a job offer!"

He'd never seen her look so excited. Mason's heart stopped in his chest as he swallowed the lump in his throat. "In New York?"

He noticed Clay grinning as April shook her head. "No, as a reporter for one of the networks that covers the PRCA rodeo circuit!"

Mason raised a brow at Clay, who shrugged and rose to hug April. "That's great, darlin'! I'm really happy for you."

"What I don't understand is that I never applied for the job."

"Well, darlin', I've heard about these headhunters that do nothing but look for good people to hire. I'll bet that's who found you."

She frowned. "I guess so. I did write a lot of articles for the college paper."

Mason smothered a grin as Clay nodded vigorously. "I bet that's it. And you know what this means, don't you? You can travel to the rodeos with me when you need to write a story, and stay here at the farm the rest of the time. We'll be one of those commuting couples, we'll work together and then we'll both live here with Mason in between competitions. Until we get big enough to hire help here, of course, then Mason can come on the road with us."

April's eyes opened wide as she turned to him. "You're staying here? You're not going back to the Army?"

"Well, I have a few months more in Germany, but yeah, after my contract is up, I think I'll be moving in here, for a while anyway. We'll see how it works out."

Clay shook his head. "Don't worry, darlin'. Once we get him here, he's never gonna leave."

"We'll see," Mason said.

"Yeah, we will." Clay hugged April harder and grinned at him over her head. "But what I'd really like to see right now is my new delivery of hay."

Mason frowned. "What are you talking about? It looks

like hay. What's to see?"

Clay's eyes twinkled. "You obviously aren't blessed with my vivid imagination. Come on, both of you. This is your home now too, and we can damn well get naked and christen the barn if we want to."

His home. That idea made Mason smile.

Christening the barn. That concept wasn't too bad, either. Mason ran to catch up with Clay and April just as he heard Clay ask, "How do you feel about rope, darlin'?"

The End

About the Author:

It all started in first grade when Cat Johnson won the essay contest at Hawthorne Elementary School and got to ride in the Chief of Police's car in the Memorial Day Parade...and the rest, as they say, is history. As an adult, Cat generally tries to stay out of police cars and is thrilled to be writing for a living. She has been published under a different name in the Young Adult genre, but Linden Bay is the first to release her romances.

On a personal note, Cat has one horse, too many cats, one dog, parakeets, fish, and a husband, and is not sure which of those gives her the most grief. Needless to say, she is very busy most days on her little 18th century farm in New York State. She plays the harp professionally and stresses that this does not mean she plays well. A past bartender, marketing manager, and Junior League president, Cat's life is quite the dichotomy, and on any given day she is just as likely to be in formal eveningwear as in mucking clothes covered in manure. Cat hates the telephone but loves email, and is looking forward to hearing from you.

cat.johnson@lindenbayromance.com

Also by Cat Johnson:

This is a publication of

Linden Bay Romance

WWW.LINDENBAYROMANCE.COM

Recommended Read:

Metamorphose by J.J. Massa
Book One - International Worlds Museum Series

*Wanting them both was one thing, having them changed
everything...*

Built on a mystic-sensitive fault, the Porta branch of the
International Worlds Museum is a busy place. Paranormal
artifacts of all kinds can be found there, magic is a way of
life, and citizens from other worlds come and go.

Wynn Ravensdale is the procurement agent for the
International Worlds Museum in the Department of Portable
Antiquities and Treasure. The epitome of propriety, Wynn
wants nothing more than to succeed at his job...except for
perhaps Leena Keene and Rand Cooper.

Wynn's roommate Leena is beautiful, brilliant, and his
twin sister's best friend. When Wynn's sister finds herself
unexpectedly a single mother, it's Leena who steps in to care
for the child. They were well on their way to fulfilling
Wynn's fantasy of becoming a happy little family. Then the
child's father, a blood drinker, showed up to reclaim what
was his, leaving Wynn severely injured.

With Ellen and the child kidnapped and Wynn in the

hospital, Rand Cooper offered help. Sexy Rand, may be rough around the edges, but his healing touch turned out to be just what Leena and Wynn needed. Together, will Rand, Leena, and Wynn find the strength, power, and love to rescue the missing and save themselves?

Printed in the United States
138866LV00004B/5/P

9 781602 021587